'You've got your D—— ——ne? Remember —— —— —— —— our mobile, bu—— —— ——l...' **Amelia's e—— —— ——ely contain his —— —— he stood waiting with her in the lobby.**

'I'll be fine,' Amelia snapped, wishing he would just be quiet. 'Might I remind you this isn't the first celebrity I've interviewed. I've delivered an article every week for the last six months.'

'But not one like this, Amelia. This has shades of your rock star Taylor Dean written all over it. Didn't he wrap up the interview by asking you to dinner?'

'This is nothing like that,' Amelia bristled, managing to simultaneously smile and give a small wave as she hissed out of the side of her mouth.

'No,' Paul responded. 'Because Vaughan Mason's got style. Have a good night.'

It was Vaughan who stepped out of the car, not his chauffeur. Vaughan who pulled open the rear door as Paul delivered his final below-the-belt remark.

'If you two aren't in bed by eleven, I want you to ring me by twelve.'

IN THE RICH MAN'S WORLD

BY
CAROL MARINELLI

MILLS & BOON®

All the characters in this book have no existence outside the imagination of the author, and have no relation whatsoever to anyone bearing the same name or names. They are not even distantly inspired by any individual known or unknown to the author, and all the incidents are pure invention.

First published in Great Britain 2005
Harlequin Mills & Boon Limited,
Eton House, 18-24 Paradise Road, Richmond, Surrey TW9 1SR

© The SAL Marinelli Family Trust 2005

ISBN 0 263 84171 5

Set in Times Roman 10½ on 12½ pt.
01-0805-43982

Printed and bound in Spain
by Litografia Rosés, S.A., Barcelona

PROLOGUE

BED.

Alone.

Just the thought of how tempting those two words sounded brought a wry smile to Vaughan's lips.

Bed alone was almost a contradiction in terms for Vaughan Mason, at least according to the journalists who tagged his every move, sensationalising every aspect of his professional dealings while attempting an angle on his private life—much to Vaughan's slightly jaundiced amusement.

Taking a belt of impossibly strong black coffee, Vaughan screwed up his nose.

He'd barely slept in thirty-six hours, had crossed several time zones and ingested enough caffeine to raise the shares of coffee beans by several per cent. All he wanted was to close his eyes on this impossibly long day, yet instead he had to face them—the journalists, the one *true* love-hate relationship in his life.

A sharp rap on his door dragged him out of his introspection. He leaned back in his chair and yawned as Katy Vale, his personal assistant, waltzed in, smiling her pussycat smile and revealing just a touch too much cleavage and thigh for a Friday afternoon as she leant over his desk and handed him a list.

'It's your lucky day.'

'I wish you'd told me that thirty-six hours ago,'

5

Vaughan retorted. His day had started at some un-godly hour in Japan and been followed by a meeting in Singapore, then several draining hours at Singapore Airport. Now, finally winding up in his office in Sydney, he felt like the sun creeping across the globe in reverse, his body clock completely kaput as jet lag finally caught up with him. The very last thing he felt like doing was being put on parade for some long-overdue interviews, but now, peering at the list, see-ing the red pen slashed through the reporters' names, he almost managed a smile.

'There's an election in the air—at least that's the buzz going around,' Katy explained. 'All the big-gun reporters have cancelled their interviews with you and flown to Canberra, trying to get their scoop…'

'Which means I can finally go to bed.'

That he had been cancelled at such short notice didn't offend Vaughan in the least—in fact it came as an unexpected pleasurable moment of relief. The Prime Minister was one of the few people who could knock him out of the headlines of the business pages, and Vaughan was only too happy to step down. The pleasure was entirely his.

Snapping the lid on his pen, he stood up and stretched. But he changed it midway into a long drawn-out sigh as Katy shook her head. 'Not just yet, I'm afraid. The *Tribune* has sent a replacement jour-nalist.'

Peering at the list, Vaughan frowned. 'Why on earth would Amelia Jacobs want to interview me?'

'You've heard of her?' Katy asked, the surprise

evident in her voice. 'Somehow I can't quite picture you reading the women's pages.'

'She's good.' Vaughan shrugged, but Katy screwed up her nose.

'She's overrated, if you ask me.'

I didn't, Vaughan almost responded, but he held his tongue. Frankly, he was too tired to be drawn into a long conversation with Katy.

Long conversations with Katy were becoming rather too frequent of late. Given any excuse, she'd sit her neat little bottom on the chair opposite and cross her perfectly toned legs, only too happy to flash her glossy smile and talk.

And could that woman talk!

What had happened to the quietly efficient woman he had hired as his PA? Where had the diligent worker who managed his impossibly tight schedule with barely a murmur gone? The woman who had glowed with pride when he'd commented on her new engagement ring, blushed with pleasure when her fiancé had arrived to pick her up?

'I mean,' Katy droned on, not remotely perturbed by his pointed silence, 'despite all the hype that surrounds her, there's not a single thing that could be described as deep about her articles; it's not as if this Amelia ever digs up the dirt on all these celebrities she interviews—there's nothing that can't be picked up in the rags...'

Vaughan suppressed a tired smile, and this time it was easier to hold back. She simply didn't get it. If Katy couldn't read between the lines that Amelia

Jacobs so skilfully crafted, then it wasn't up to him to point it out.

Amelia Jacobs was a master.

Or mistress.

Or whatever the politically correct term was these days.

Amelia Jacobs had, in the few months she'd been writing for the paper, developed something of a cult following—a group of loyal readers who read her articles with their tongues placed firmly in cheek, perhaps sharing a wry smile with a fellow devotee as they glimpsed over the top of their newspaper in some café or airport lounge.

Amelia Jacobs, in Vaughan's not so humble opinion, had her finger on the pulse, but wasn't afraid to remove it when needed, to stray from the usual run-of-the-mill questions and delve a little deeper, to somehow get her subjects to finally confirm or deny the rumours that plagued them. Her interviews were a strange mix of cynicism and compassion.

'Why does she want to interview me?' Vaughan asked again, then corrected himself. Every journalist this side of the equator seemed to want a piece of him, but the fact he had neither dreadlocks nor body piercings, actually managed to eat and keep down three meals a day, and didn't have a father who'd abused him, didn't put Vaughan in the usual category of Amelia Jacobs's subjects. 'Or rather, why do you think I'd want to be interviewed by her?'

'Because you are always in the news for all the wrong reasons,' Katy responded in a matter-of-fact voice. 'There was that supermodel, the actress…'

'Definitely no bishop, though,' Vaughan clipped back, but even his dry humour didn't allow him to dodge the uncomfortable issue.

Uncomfortable because suddenly discussing his sex life with Katy seemed like a very bad idea indeed.

'That was all over ages ago,' he said finally, staring coolly back as Katy rearranged her crossed legs, smiling sweetly over at him as he protested his rather recent innocence.

'I know,' Katy soothed. 'But you know what the press can be like once they've got the bit between their teeth. And you don't need me to tell you that you haven't exactly been the blue-eyed boy...'

'I don't,' Vaughan said, with a slightly warning edge to his voice.

Katy cleared her throat again. 'It was agreed at the last directors' meeting that if the opportunity came then you should show the media that there's a softer side to you.'

'But there isn't.' Vaughan shrugged. 'What you see is what you get.'

'I don't agree.' Dropping her voice, she stared back at him, flicking her hair away from her pretty face with her left hand, and Vaughan felt his heart plummet—the absence of her engagement ring was vividly noticeable for the very first time. 'Look how nice you were to me when I broke up with Andy.'

'I didn't realise you had.' Vaughan gave a very on-off smile, watching in slightly bored horror as she smiled over at him, from under her lashes now. He felt a subtle shift in the room that most men would miss—but Vaughan read women as easily as a recipe book, and while he'd been away Katy had clearly lined up all her ingredients and was right now stirring the pot and about to offer him a taste!

'We broke up a couple of weeks ago. It hurt a lot at the time, but I guess I'm starting to move on.' Boldly she held his gaze. 'Why don't you come over for dinner tonight, Vaughan? I'm sure cooking is the last thing you want to do now, and you must have had your fill of restaurants.'

'Thanks, but no thanks.' Vaughan deflected her offer easily, quite sure he wasn't hungry—on either count! 'I just want to go to bed.'

God, she was bold. A tiny smile twitched on well-made-up lips at the mere mention of the word, and she was still holding his gaze. Vaughan knew exactly what was on the menu—knew that if he took her up on the offer they wouldn't be starting at the entrée, instead they'd be bypassing the main course and moving directly to dessert!

Watching her face drop as he firmly shook his head and picked up his pen, Vaughan consoled himself that he was doing her a favour really—if he slept with her he'd end up firing her!

'Send Miss Jacobs in as soon as she arrives—and,' he added firmly, 'once she gets here you might as well go home.'

'I don't mind waiting,' Katy persisted, but Vaughan was insistent.

'Go home, Katy.' He didn't soften his rejection with a smile, didn't even look up from his work. Mixed messages were clearly not what were needed here. 'I'll catch up with you in Melbourne next week.'

CHAPTER ONE

SEND.

Amelia's finger hovered over the computer key, then pulled back.

She made a quick dash into the bathroom, and inhaled the delicious scent of bergamot mixing perfectly with frankincense and just an undertone of lavender. Her Friday afternoon routine was written in stone:

Read her article as objectively as possible.

Clean the flat while all the time reciting paragraphs of article out loud, adding mental commas and meaningful exclamation marks.

Head into the high street while still mulling over article.

Drop off dry cleaning.

Stop for a café latté—extra-strength with full-cream milk and three sugars.

Head for home.

Finish article, adding said commas and exclamation marks.

Take phone off the hook and run bath.

Finally hit 'send' and, as her work drifted into cyberspace, dive into the awaiting aromatic bath, allowing the fragrance to soothe. Lavender was supposedly fabulous for stress headaches, and for

11

the past six months, come Friday at four p.m., a stress headache was exactly what she'd had.

Okay, her article would still make the deadline if she sent it at five, but she needed that hour. Needed to lie in her fabulous bubbly bath as the blood, sweat and tears she'd shed over the past seven days wafted through cyberspace and into her editor Paul's in-box. Needed that hour wallowing in the bath forgetting the horrors she'd been through the past week.

Sure, interviewing celebrities, eating out at fabulous restaurants and actually being paid to write about it sounded like most people's dream job come true. But for Amelia it was merely a means to an end. Contracted on a freelance basis to cover a nine-month maternity leave position, Amelia had taken the job with the sole intention of making a name for herself, networking with the right people, and hopefully— *hopefully*—landing a more permanent position in the offices on the second floor, the hallowed ground of the business reporters. There she would be writing not about the rise and fall of celebrities' bustlines or their latest off-on romances, but about the far more intriguing effect of rises and falls on world stock markets, or the impact of the US dollar on trading in Australia, and hopefully one day she'd get an inside scoop on a major business deal which would surely seal her arrival as a heavyweight. And maybe would even win her father's approval!

But so far nothing had happened. Sure, her editor, Paul, had made all the right noises—insisted he was talking to people behind the scenes as he handed

Amelia her latest task for the week. But still nothing had happened, and with Maria's maternity leave galloping into the final run Amelia was starting to feel more than a touch anxious. Not just because of the lack of movement in the business side of things, but because she'd grown rather used to having a regular wage in the fickle world of journalism. She also had to admit it was because she'd be leaving a job she'd started to love…

Closing her eyes, Amelia let out the breath she'd been inadvertently holding, half expecting that if she opened her eyes she'd see her father's appalled expression at the fact that the daughter of Grant Jacobs, esteemed political reporter, could possibly *like* writing such articles, could actually *enjoy* interviewing celebrities, confirming or denying salacious rumours and feeding the never-ending quest for insight into Australia's most beautiful.

He'd never call it news!

With the soapy water now licking the edges of her claw-foot bath, Amelia twisted off the taps, ran into the lounge, which tripled as a dining room and study, and turned on her favorite CD. She listened as the decadent, fabulous voice of Robbie told her that once he found her he'd never let her go, and finally she did relax.

The phone was off the hook—as it always was when she'd finished a piece—her horoscope was waiting to be read, and a glass of chilled white wine was by the bath.

Routine firmly in place, she took a deep breath and, with her hand over the send key, closed her eyes and pressed it. Then, as she did every Friday, she ran like the wind into her tiny cramped bathroom, stripped off in record time, and winced as she submerged herself into too-hot water. She waited for her body to acclimatize and her over-sized boobs to waft up onto the surface, waiting for their owner to pluck up the guts to sink fully into the water. She would massage that deep heated conditioner that promised miracles into her hair, then lie back and read her horoscope just as she always did.

A fabulous period supposedly lay ahead. Virgos should be ready to embrace changes, throw caution to the wind and take up crazy offers, arming themselves for opportunity, getting ready to expect the unexpected and let a little romance shine into their lives.

For once Louis the astrologer had got it wrong.

Turning to the front of the magazine, Amelia stared at the scowling face of Taylor Dean, every inch the popstar, walking out of a chic restaurant, the requisite beautiful woman firmly entrenched on his arm. She was scarcely able to comprehend that six months ago it had been she, Amelia, on that arm.

Perhaps Louis had misplaced his notes—accidentally repeated her July horoscope in the middle of January—because six months ago today a fabulous period really had lain ahead. The crazy offer of a date with Taylor had literally fallen into her lap, and she'd been foolish enough to accept—stupid and naive enough to throw caution to the wind and let a little romance into her life. Only where had it got her?

Staring into Taylor's brown eyes, Amelia felt as if she were choking on her own humiliation—remembering with total recall the shattered remains their whirlwind romance had left in its wake and the almost impossible task of rebuilding her professional reputation. Colleagues had been only too happy to believe that every scoop she got, every inside piece of information she was privy to, must somehow have been gleaned between the sheets.

But she'd learnt from her mistake.

For the following five months she'd been with the *Tribute* Amelia had been the epitome of professionalism. All her articles had been in before their deadline, she had researched her subjects carefully, and, though friendly and personable, she had maintained a respectable distance, despite a couple of rather surprising offers, determined that by the time Maria returned from her maternity leave Taylor Dean would be a vague memory.

At least in her editor Paul's eyes!

Tears she simply refused to shed were blinked firmly back and the magazine tossed onto the floor. Taylor's features blurred as a sympathetic puddle on the floor licked at the front page—only not quickly enough for Amelia. Taylor's cheating eyes were still staring out at her, the wounds he had inflicted on her once-trusting heart still too raw not to hurt when touched, and she gave up on her relaxing bath, pulled out the plug and padded into the living room.

'No!'

Her wail went unheard as, standing shivering in a towel, she saw her computer—despite frantic pressing of Control-Alt-Delete, remain frozen. Its only movement was a red sign appearing, warning of Trojan horses galloping towards her and worms poking their heads out of the woodwork at the most inopportune time.

'*No!*' she wailed again, dragging a chair over with her wrinkled bath-soaked foot and with chattering teeth trying to wrestle with the unforgiving screen of her computer.

It was twenty to five!

Thoughts of Paul's reaction were the only thing that ran through Amelia's mind as she rang her computer guru—only to be told that it was happening to everyone, that computers were crashing with more speed than a pile-up on a freeway.

If she missed the deadline...she'd be dead!

Not even bothering to replace the receiver, not even remembering to thank him, Amelia gulped in air, picturing the scenario. Okay, the piece she was filing so urgently today wouldn't actually appear until next week's colour supplement, but in the cut-throat world of journalism deadlines came second only to a pulse.

First, actually.

Without fulfilling one's deadlines, your pulse didn't even matter.

She could almost see Paul's raised eyebrow as she stammered her way through an apology. Could almost feel the breeze from his dismissive wave as he assured her it didn't matter a jot, that of course this was a one-off and they'd naturally take into consideration when deciding her fate that every other piece she'd filed had been delivered before deadline...

No problem, Amelia. He'd smile. *Don't worry about it, Amelia,* he'd say, waving away her stammering excuses. *These things happen to the best of us.*

Oh, he'd make all the right noises, insist that it didn't really matter, while simultaneously checking with Personnel just how long it would be till the impossibly efficient Maria came back.

A whimper of horror escaped Amelia's chattering lips as she pressed every last key on her computer, watching with mounting horror as each page she attempted to open froze on top of the other, as words dropped like autumn leaves from her screen, replaced instead with the horror of empty white squares on empty white squares, as the stupid, defunct, way-too-late virus warning alerted her of impending doom.

Doom!

Raking fingers through aromatic oiled hair that badly needed a rinse, she squeezed a breath into her lungs.

Back-up.

'Please…' Amelia whimpered, pushing the eject button on her computer and pulling out the disc. Thank God she'd remembered to press 'save'! If she got dressed now, forgot make-up and managed to hail a cab in record time, she'd be just ten minutes late.

Rummaging through her wardrobe, berating the fact that her usual boxy suits were all stacked in a pile at the dry cleaners, Amelia pulled on some weekend jeans and pushed her damp body into a sheer lilac top that, had time allowed, would definitely have benefited from a bra. But time was of the essence. Hailing a cab, she dragged a comb through her short, spiky blonde hair as she rattled around on the back seat, making vague conversation with the driver and attempting a slick of mascara as they swung into George Street.

She was ready to hand over her disk to Clara the receptionist with a quick smile and then beat a hasty retreat, absolutely determined not to be caught looking anything other than the smart, efficient, businesswoman she always portrayed.

'Amelia!' Mumbling into the phone receiver she was holding, Clara blew her fringe skywards and gave a grateful smile. 'Thank goodness you're here.'

Never had Clara seemed so pleased to see her. More to the point, never had Clara even grunted a greeting—her efficient smile was reserved for *real* journalists, the ones whose stories actually mattered, not some two-bit freelancer who appeared in the Saturday colour supplement.

'I'm only ten minutes late,' Amelia mumbled, pushing the shiny silver disk across the desk and glancing at the clock above Clara's head, praying it was going faster than her watch. 'I'm normally on time—I'm usually early…'

'Don't worry about that,' Clara said, screwing up her nose as she picked up the disk and, to Amelia's horror, tossed it into a drawer. 'Didn't you hear the news?'

'News?' Amelia gave a bewildered blink, cursing herself that the one time in the week she turned off the radio, the one time she let the world disappear to concentrate on a piece, something had really happened.

'There might be an election! Friday afternoon's a

lousy time to call for a press conference if you ask me, but that's what's happened.'

Another bewildered blink from Amelia before excitement started to mount. Images of serious pieces with her name on them drifted into her mind, but before they had even formed Clara easily doused them.

'Which means all the big names are tied up.'

'Amelia!' Paul, her editor, appeared at the lift doors. He handed her a file as he juggled a call on his mobile and his pager bleeped loudly. 'Carter has had to fly to Canberra…'

'I heard,' Amelia replied as Paul decided the call on his mobile was more important. She flicked open the folder he had pressed in her hand for something to do, then caught her breath—not for the first time today, but for an entirely different reason.

Vaughan Mason.

That inscrutable face was actually smiling at her from a black and white photo, but even with the healing balm of a soft-focus lens the slightly cruel twist to his full mouth was still evident. The black eyes stared back unnervingly, a dark jet fringe flopping over one superbly carved eyebrow. His unshaven, heavily shadowed jaw would have been more in place in a sports calendar than on a business shoot, but apart from that his utter supremacy screamed from every pore. Even the glimpse of his suit in the head-and-shoulders shot reeked of abhorrent wealth, and suddenly her horoscope made sense. Suddenly Venus was aligning with Pluto—or was it Uranus?—and the heavenly changes Louis had faithfully promised, no, warned her to be prepared for were really happening.

'Carter had a fifteen-minute spot with him,' Paul mouthed as he covered the mouthpiece on his mobile.

'When?'

'In twenty minutes' time. You're the fill-in.'

'Me?'

Paul nodded and, possibly realising the urgency of the situation, put his caller on hold. 'You'll be great, Amelia, you always are. I don't know how you do it, but somehow you manage to reel them in, get them to show their true colours, just like you did with Taylor Dean….' Seeing her paling face, Paul changed tack. 'As good as Carter is, he'd never have even attempted your angle.'

'What sort of angle are you looking for?' Amelia asked, Paul's insensitive words having hit a very raw nerve.

'The man behind the millions—what makes his cold heart tick…'

'Nothing?' Amelia ventured, but Paul shook his head.

'We've got a big story about to break on him. You could be the perfect lead-in. I'll suggest that we hold next Saturday's middle pages for it.'

'Middle pages…' Amelia repeated, her face paling. 'Of the paper, not the…?'

'The paper,' Paul confirmed. 'If you're sure you're up to it.'

'Oh, I'm up to it,' Amelia responded quickly, with way more confidence than she felt. 'What sort of story's about to break? Do you think he's going to pull off the motor deal?'

'Oh, it's bigger than the motor deal,' Paul responded, unable to stop a small boast, but changing his mind at the last moment. 'Trust me, Amelia. The less you know, the better—he's sharp enough to know if you're fishing for information. Just dazzle him the way you did Taylor…'

'I'll have to get changed,' Amelia broke in, determined not to go there. Glancing down at her jean-clad legs and bare arms, she knew she couldn't face Vaughan Mason dressed like this. But Paul was already frog-marching her through Reception

'There isn't time for all that.' Paul shook his head firmly. 'Vaughan Mason won't be kept waiting—you'll just have to go as you are.' His reassuring smile rapidly disappeared as for the first time he took in her dishevelled appearance, giving a rather noticeable frown as he eyed her jeans and sandals. 'Frankly, Amelia, I expected better from you. Maria would never have—'

'I had no idea I'd be doing an interview this afternoon,' Amelia attempted. 'I only came by to drop off my article.'

'You're supposed to expect the unexpected,' Paul countered, sounding like her wretched horoscope. 'That's what journalism is all about.'

And he was right, Amelia conceded through gritted teeth. If it had been any other hour of any other day she'd have been ready—more than ready for the challenge. If only she had listened to her horoscope! If she had she wouldn't be standing here totally unprepared for the biggest break in her career.

'I want you to come back to the office after the interview and let me know how it went. I've pulled this from Carter's desk.' He held out another very thin folder.

'I thought you said he had something on him?' Amelia rolled her eyes. 'Don't tell me—that's for Carter's eyes only. What's in here?'

'Facts and figures,' Paul admitted. 'Have a quick read on the way—but, Amelia, try not to focus too much on the business side. Work your magic on him, see if you can get him to open up a bit about his family, his personal life…'

'His women?' Amelia rolled her eyes again.

Vaughan Mason's reputation was legendary. Pages and pages of the glossies had been filled over the years with tear-streaked gorgeous faces, broken promises and shattered hearts—seemingly the price for a night in this man's company. But through all the scandals, through all the revelations, Vaughan had remained tight-lipped, repeatedly refusing to comment. And his lack of excuses, his utter refusal to be drawn or, heaven forbid, to apologise, had only served to make women want him more.

'I'm hardly likely to get him to open up in a fifteen-minute time slot…' Amelia started, but a warning look from Paul had her voice trailing off. There was no room for negativity in the cut-throat world of journalism. 'It will be great, Paul—just great. You're not going to regret this.'

'I hope not.' Paul's eyes narrowed a fraction.

'Maria's going to be devastated that she missed this opportunity.'

Maria.

The one name that said it all. The one word that reminded her of the very temporary nature of her position

She had to get it right.

Had to do as her horoscope said and embrace the opportunity. Had to somehow get noticed. So that next time the sniff of an election was in the air she'd be heading to Canberra, not standing in a humid, muggy Sydney street, attempting to hail a taxi in the middle of Friday-night rush hour and trying to call around and find out Vaughan Mason's latest value on the stock market.

Meticulous research was Amelia's forte.

That was how she got celebrities to open up.

Flattery heaped on flattery—it worked every time.

Watching appalling films, reading even worse biographies, seducing stars with her insight! But how was she supposed to woo Vaughan when all her research was being done in the back of taxi hurtling through the city at breakneck speed towards a subject she knew nothing about other than the undeniable ruthlessness of his business dealings that had been reported in the newspapers, coupled with regular romance scandals that found their way into the glossies?

Gulping in the stuffy air, Amelia skimmed the facts and figures neatly typed in the folder in her lap, silently appalled that one man could hold so much wealth and power.

From what she could ascertain not a single cent of

his millions strayed from his path. Normally a list of charities appeared in bios, in an attempt to soften the figures and show that there was a warmer side to a ruthless personality. Normally a few family shots appeared, or a snippet of personal information—a small sideline on hobbies or interests—but, thanks to Carter, all the file on Vaughan Mason contained were cold, hard business facts. How he'd built his massive wealth from the ground upwards, how he'd saved flailing businesses over and over, forging a reputation on gut feeling and confidence alone!

She could hardly quote the glossies to him! How was she supposed to get a different angle when there wasn't one?

Paying the taxi driver, she stared upwards at the impressive tower before her, scarcely able to believe she was really here. Catching sight of her reflection in a glass window, Amelia let out a low moan—the humid Sydney air had done nothing to accelerate her hair-drying and, glancing down at her watch, she wished for the umpteenth time that she could dart into a boutique and buy something—anything other than what she was wearing. That she could greet this demi-god if not on his level at least in smart clothes.

Maybe it would work in her favour, Amelia consoled herself, flashing her ID at an immaculate, very suitably dressed woman who might have been Clara Mark Two and being shown to a lift out of sight of the main reception area. She showed her ID again, to a gentleman who had more muscles than your average body builder and didn't even attempt conversation, then her stomach was left on the ground as the lift soared to the heavens, towards the very man himself.

'Miss Jacobs?'

Yet another clone of Clara was greeting her, but this one introduced herself as Katy, rouged smile firmly in place. Even with a few mils of Botox injected into her forehead this one couldn't quite hide her surprise at the scruffy-looking woman who had appeared in the office.

'Mr Mason's ready for you. I'll just let him know that you're here.' Picking up the phone, she spoke in low soothing tones, clearly for Vaughan's ears only. 'Well, if you're sure,' she soothed, purring into the phone. 'In that case I'll see you in Melbourne next Friday. Have a safe flight.' She turned her gaze to Amelia. 'He said to go right in.'

'Thank you.' Amelia nodded crisply, attempting blasé, but nerves finally caught up. 'Could I just use the powder room first?'

'Of course.'

Even the powder room was gorgeous: white marble everywhere, pump-action soap that was actually full, expensive moisturiser, and a mirror that was way too large in Amelia's present state. Still, she turned on the hand-dryer full blast and attempted to dry her hair, but to no avail—the heavy waft of lavender as the dryer met her damp hair did nothing to soothe Amelia now! She'd just have to put on her best smile and hope for the best…

Walking back into Reception, Amelia nodded to Katy, who was slowly pulling on her jacket, clearly reluctant to leave her boss in anyone's hands but her own. Knocking on the door, Amelia swallowed hard, forced a bright confident smile and pushed back her shoulders—not quite as ready as she'd have liked for the biggest moment of her career, but excited all the same.

'Mr Mason? I'm Amelia Jacobs…' She strode confidently forward, just as she had rehearsed during the taxi ride, hand outstretched. Her eyes scanned the room in a nano-second, her voice trailing off as her footsteps did the same, staring in utter disbelief at the sight that greeted her.

Vaughan Mason—business tycoon, eternally vigilant man of stealth—lay asleep on the jade leather couch.

Asleep.

And what made it even more inappropriate was how completely stunning he looked.

Dark lashes fanned the even darker rims under his eyes; razor-sharp cheekbones emphasised the hollows of his face. His unshaven chin was for once not set in stone, and that cruel, full mouth was unfamiliar in its relaxed state, lips slightly parted. His tie was askew, shifted to one side, and the bottom of his very white Egyptian-cotton shirt was inching its way out of an expensively belted waistband.

She was assailed with the most inappropriate of feelings, given the circumstance, and felt an almost instinctive need to reach out and touch him, as one might a work of art finally witnessed first hand—to feel the scratch of his stubble beneath her fingers, the cool marble of his skin. His beauty truly daunted her. Not a blemish marred his skin. The only fault, if you could call it that, was the too severe, almost too dark, eyebrows—yet even they seemed fitting somehow, as if some pensive artist had added them, and was waiting in the wings with a charcoaled thumb poised ready to blend them in further the moment she left.

Amelia had the most inappropriate urge to lean over and press her mouth against his, to feel those full lips under hers, to sneak a kiss when no one was looking, climb over the imaginary thick red ropes that separated art from mortals, ignore the mental signs that said 'Do Not Touch'. And though she never would have dared, never in a million years, it was like standing on a cliff face and wanting to jump—knowing it was treacherous, knowing it would prove fatal, but filled with a yearning all the same to throw caution to the wind and follow natural instincts.

Shaking her head fiercely, pushing impossible thoughts away, she felt a moment of sheer panic.

Panic!

And it didn't compare to the computer virus, nor even to anything she'd ever experienced in her life to this point.

She didn't know what to do—literally didn't know what to do.

Shake him, perhaps? Or go out and knock more loudly this time, pretend she'd never even witnessed this magnate in an off-guard moment?

But why should she? Amelia thought with a flash of anger. Why should she make things more comfortable for him? Why was she standing here feeling embarrassed when it should be Vaughan Mason squirming with shame and embarrassment? Sure, he dealt with journalists all the time, and everyone knew he didn't stand on ceremony for them, but she'd bet her bottom dollar that if it had been Carter doing the interview instead of her then Vaughan Mason would have at least had the decency to stay awake.

This was the biggest moment in her career—literally make or break—and bloody Vaughan Mason had the audacity to sleep through her entrance, had the temerity to doze off before her questions had even started, and relegate her to the struggling novice she was without a single word!

'Mr Mason,' Amelia said loudly, burning with humiliation and anger, stupid, stupid tears pricking her eyes. 'Mr Mason!'

Navy eyes peeped open—navy eyes that stared directly at her, that ignited something she couldn't at that moment identify. But it spun her further into unfamiliar disorder—her pulse-rate accelerating, her anger fanning as he had the audacity to stretch and yawn, not even bothering to cover his mouth.

'Sorry about that,' he said, not sounding remotely so, in the deep voice she'd heard during numerous appearances on the news and radio. 'I must have dozed off.'

'Oh, you didn't "doze off",' Amelia retorted, scarcely able to believe the provocation behind her own response. The consummate professional, she usually smiled through everything—yet for reasons she couldn't even begin to fathom here she was answering back when she should stay quiet, letting her subject know exactly what she thought of his appalling behaviour when she should just let it go. 'You were asleep, Mr Mason. Sound asleep. Snoring, in fact, when we're supposed to be doing an interview.'

'I don't snore,' he said easily, throwing incredibly long legs over the edge of the couch and bringing himself to a stand, tucking in his shirt and then towering over her, somehow instantly regaining control. 'Had you arrived on time the interview would have been over with by now…' He glanced at his watch—or rather he didn't glance. Glances happened in a split second, whereas Vaughan positively stared, letting out a long held-in breath as the second hand ticked loudly on. Twisting his mouth into the cruel smile she knew so well, he said, 'And, had you arrived on time, Miss Jacobs, I can assure that you'd have found me awake.'

It was Amelia running her fingers through her own hair now, colour flaming in her pale cheeks as she felt the oily mass that greeted her fingers, felt the unspoken derision in the flicker of his gaze as he dragged his eyes the length of her body.

Her editor's gaze had been derisive, and she'd dealt with it, Amelia reminded herself, but her body burned with shame as she felt Vaughan slowly take in her brightly painted toenails, her naked feet slipped into silver sandals. The faded jeans that had seen better days merited a raised eyebrow that spoke volumes, and she felt a scorch of further humiliation as he languorously lifted his gaze and stopped, she was sure, at breasts that moved unhindered as her breathing quickened. Breasts that were still damp and heavy from her bath, straining at the leash under her softly ruched top. Way, way too big for an outing into this office without the firm support of a bra. Even Paul had told her to her face that she was inappropriately dressed, but though it had stung it hadn't really mattered. Nothing from Paul could begin to compare to the sting of Vaughan's disapproval as his eyes finally sought her face.

'Your appointment was for five.' Staring down again at his preposterously expensive watch, he frowned with concentration. 'It's now nearly twenty past.'

She should have apologised, Amelia knew—*knew* that was what she should do. Hell, it wasn't as if Vaughan Mason was the first of her subjects to behave atrociously. She'd been left stranded at restaurant tables more times than she could remember when her interviewee had failed to show, had waited patiently for celebrity 'naturally thin' new mothers to return from the powder room between each course more times than she could count. She'd even had subjects fall asleep mid-sentence, come to that!

So why was she overreacting now? Why wasn't she swallowing this bitter pill with the sweetest of smiles and attempting to redeem what was left of this awful situation? Why wasn't she attempting to implement some sort of rescue plan? But it was as if her foot was stuck on an emotional accelerator; she could almost smell the petrol fumes as her mouth opened and she revved up again.

'I'm well aware of the contempt in which you hold journalists, Mr Mason.' Holding up his bio with slightly shaking hands, she attempted to fix him with a firm stare of her own. 'And I'm more than aware that I'd be flattering myself to imagine that fifteen minutes in my company might cause you even the slightest twinge of anxiety. But this happens to be extremely important to me, and to walk in and find you sound asleep…' She struggled for eloquence, attempting to swallow the shrill ring that was rising in her voice, to finish her argument with some crushing words that would shame him into submission. But settled instead for the only two words that sprang to her dizzy, emotional mind. 'How *rude*!'

'I wasn't *sound* asleep,' he said, his cool, utterly controlled voice the antithesis of hers. 'But funny you should say that when I was thinking exactly the same thing myself.' His mouth twisted into that familiar cruel smile. 'I was just thinking how *rude* it was of the newspaper to cancel at such short notice, how *rude* it was of them to send a replacement journalist without having the courtesy to first run it by me…'

'Your PA approved it—' Amelia started, but her voice faded mid-sentence as Vaughan overrode her.

'Indeed she did,' Vaughan clipped. 'Though no doubt at the time she was expecting a rather more suitable replacement.'

'So, were you expecting one of the bigger names?' Amelia bristled, but Vaughan shook his head.

'Oh, no, Miss Jacobs. I was told it was you that would be doing the interview.'

'Then why…?' Confused, she blinked back at him. Her mouth opened to ask what he meant, but quickly she closed it again, shame coursing through her as realisation hit home and she braced herself for a dressing-down Mason style. And Vaughan took great pleasure in confirming his displeasure at her attitude and attire, nailing his answer with a brutality that was as savage as it was legendary.

'*Rude!*' He said the word slowly, rolled it slowly out of full lips, his face impassive.

Amelia's cheeks flamed, and she swallowed hard under his scrutiny, wishing he would just get it over with so she could get the hell out of there. Clearly this interview wasn't going to happen, but Vaughan wasn't rushing. Her allotted time-slot might be well and truly over, but Vaughan Mason wasn't in any hurry to finish, mentally circling her like a vulture over his prey as the single word resonated in the air.

'Impolite, uncouth, inappropriate…' His forehead frowned slowly. 'Did my lying on the couch while I awaited your arrival offend you that much, Miss Jacobs?' He didn't await her answer; she'd never really expected him to. 'We must have a different understanding of the word.' He flashed a tiny smile that didn't meet his eyes, in fact he barely moved his lips. '*Rude* is arriving in my office with wet hair and inappropriate clothes. *Rude* is barging in here completely unprepared…'

'How do you know that I'm unprepared? How do you know that I haven't got a list of pertinent—?' Amelia attempted, but Vaughan shot her down in an instant, picking up a newspaper from his desk and waving it at her.

'Had you read your own newspaper you'd know that I've been on the go non-stop for the last thirty-six hours. That before I went to Singapore I had a prolonged stopover in Japan, meeting with Mr Cheng and drinking endless cups of green tea while trying to broker a deal that will bring jobs and dollars to this country and hopefully save a flailing industry that most people have written off.'

'I know about the motor deal you're attempting,' Amelia responded. 'In fact I've been monitoring it closely. I know that in a few weeks' time you're hoping to…'

'I move quickly, Miss Jacobs. And, had you been more professional from the outset, you might have been the first to find out…' His voice trailed off and Amelia watched in something akin to disbelief as Vaughan appeared to flounder, giving a tiny shake of his head, as if he couldn't quite believe what he had just revealed.

'It's about to go through?' Her voice was an incredulous whisper, her green eyes widening as she processed this piece of front-page news; everyone had said it was an impossible feat, a war that quite simply couldn't be won even if the David that faced Goliath happened to be Vaughan Mason. 'You've actually managed to pull it off?'

But it wasn't only Amelia's mind that was working overtime. Amelia wasn't the only one reeling at the snippet of information he had so easily imparted.

Vaughan quite simply couldn't believe it himself. Already embarrassed at being caught asleep, he could scarcely believe he had mentally relaxed twice in a row. His defences were eternally up, yet one moment in this woman's company and he had felt them waver. Her sparkling green eyes had caught him completely off guard—eyes that seemed to stare not at him but through him, through to somewhere deep inside, where no one was permitted. He had given this woman, this stranger, this *journalist* an opening, a chance to destroy what he had spent months building, and Vaughan knew that he had to somehow retrieve it, had to somehow pull sharply back, get her the hell out of here just as fast as he could.

'Repeat what I just said and I'll sue.' Direct, threatening and straight to the point.

Vaughan felt himself retrieve the grip he had momentarily lost and watched her face pale before him, utter despair filling those expressive eyes as he snatched back the tidbit he had so readily thrown. 'I think you should leave now.'

Amelia opened her mouth to argue, then closed it again, perhaps realising it would be futile, and Vaughan let out a breath of relief as without further ado she headed for the door.

And that should have been it. If it had been anyone else he was sure this rather uncomfortable exchange would be over by now, so why did she have to go and turn around? Why couldn't she have just cut her losses and got the hell out?

'I'm sorry.'

For Amelia, the apology that had spilled from her mouth was as unexpected as it was genuine. She'd meant to just leave—had fully intended to slam the door on this insufferable man. But with a stab of cruel honesty she realised that her anger was misdirected, that the only person who'd blown her chance was herself. Tears that had no place if she wanted to escape with her last withering shred of dignity were held firmly back and she gave a small shake of her head in defeat.

'I *have* been rude, appallingly so, and the truth of the matter is I've no idea why.' She gave a tiny shrug. 'You're right. I have just come out of the bath and I'm woefully inappropriately dressed. I had the phone off the hook because I was working on an important piece.' Amelia gave a dry laugh. 'Well, it seemed important at the time. Then my computer got a virus…'

Her voice trailed off. Vaughan Mason didn't need details. An apology was the only thing needed now.

'Had I had any idea prior to five p.m. that I'd be interviewing you, Mr Mason, then I'd have spent every available minute researching you and would have arrived in the smartest of suits. I had no right to barge in here all accusatory. I was just…'

Again, she struggled for eloquence but gave in, words literally failing her, unable to justify even to herself what had just taken place, secretly hoping he'd put her out of her misery, end the torture she'd started and let her go meekly on her way. But Vaughan had other ideas.

'Just what?'

'Overwhelmed.' Amelia chewed on her lip as she struggled to find the words. 'I'm usually incredibly ordered. OCD is my middle name…' He didn't even laugh at her rather feeble joke. 'Obsessive compulsive disorder…'

'I know what OCD is.'

'I pride myself on being prepared, and when I found out I was interviewing you I guess I just panicked. I've been trying to move into business report-ing, and had I handled it better this really could have been a huge break for me.' Forcing a brave smile, she offered her hand. 'I've already taken up enough of your time. Once again, I really am sorry.'

As his expression softened a shade she almost dared to hope that he'd refuse her hand and, with a nod of that immaculately cut hair, relent and gesture for her to come in. But that vague hope was doused before it had even formed: after only the briefest of hesitations Vaughan Mason's warm, dry hand closed around hers.

'What will you say? I mean, what will you write?'

'My notice, probably, when I return to the office empty-handed.' Amelia sighed, but emotional black-mail clearly didn't move Vaughan Mason an inch. He just stood there as Amelia turned and pulled the heavy door open. 'Congratulations, by the way.' She saw the flicker of confusion in his tired eyes, realised only then just how exhausted he must be if a billion-dollar deal could so easily be forgotten. 'On the contract.'

'Oh, that!' He gave a tight nod. 'Thanks. Although it's a touch premature. It's far from in the bag, and, as I said—'

'Off the record, or you'll sue?' Amelia second-guessed him and gave a wan smile. 'Don't worry; my next piece will be called "You heard it here *last*".'

She slipped out of his office and into the hallway. The elevator must have been expecting her, because it slid open before she even approached, killing stone-dead any lingering hope that he might change his mind, might pull open the door and call her back in.

As if.

As if Vaughan Mason would even give their altercation a second thought.

Stepping out onto the street, she ignored the taxi rank and decided instead to walk. What was the point of rushing to the gallows?

She could almost see Paul's thunderous face when she told him what had happened. Could imagine her bank balance sliding into the red as she struggled to find another gig.

The one major scoop of her life had practically been gift-wrapped and handed to her on a plate, and she'd somehow managed to mess it up.

But it wasn't just her lack of journalistic acumen causing Amelia's feet to drag. Glancing back over her shoulder, she stared up at the ostentatious high-rise building, squinting into the low, late-afternoon sun at the black-tinted windows, remembering Vaughan lying asleep on the couch... And she was suddenly assailed with regret of a rather more personal nature.

If only she'd dared kiss him!

CHAPTER TWO

'PAUL said you were to go straight through,' Clara greeted her. 'And by the way he's not in the sunniest of moods.'

Perhaps he already knew. Amelia sighed, picking her way through the practically empty office and knocking wearily on his door. Perhaps Vaughan had wasted no time picking up the telephone and complaining to her senior about the poor replacement he had sent.

Oh, well, if nothing else it would save her the indignity of repeating the debacle; living through it the first time had been bad enough

As usual Paul was on the telephone.

As usual he gestured for her to sit, with barely a glance, and sit Amelia did—nausea rising with every breath and the oppressive scent of a large bouquet of stunning orchids which adorned Paul's desk doing nothing to help.

'How did it go?' Paul finally asked, hanging up the telephone and scribbling down a few notes. 'Oh, and these came for you,' he added when Amelia didn't immediately answer, pushing the bouquet forward, watching her strained face as she fingered the pale pink waxy petals. 'Most women would die to be in your position, you know? Most women would give their right arm to have Taylor Dean constantly sending them flowers and begging for forgiveness.'

'No, Paul, they wouldn't,' Amelia sighed, wishing Taylor would just drop it, wishing his ego could finally admit that it was over and he'd realise that for once in his life he wasn't going to be forgiven his sins.

'What's he got to say for himself this time?'

Amelia didn't need to read the card to find out—no doubt it was another ream of excuses, another plea for forgiveness.

'So, how did it go with Mason?' Paul asked again, returning to his notes. And, given that it was the second time he'd asked, given that Paul didn't like to be kept waiting, Amelia knew that her tiny reprieve was over. The curtain was lifting and the final act was about to begin

'Not very well.' She watched the smile wiped from Paul's face, watched as his pen froze over the paper and he instantly reverted from colleague to boss.

'Which means exactly what?'

Amelia swallowed hard, peeling open the envelope from the bouquet for something to do. Taylor's pathetic excuses were preferable to Paul's harsh, direct stare.

'He wasn't really up to an interview. He was tired…'

'Vaughan Mason's never tired,' Paul hissed. 'Vaughan Mason isn't a mere mortal who needs six hours' sleep to function, like the rest of us…'

'He *was* tired,' Amelia insisted, pulling the card out of the envelope and glancing down at the writing—anything other than meeting her boss's eyes. 'He's just flown back from Asia…'

'Did you find out anything about the motor vehicle deal?'

For a second she wavered. For a second integrity seemed a poor buffer against the harsh reality of a world without work. But unfortunately it must have been indelibly implanted, because after only the briefest of pauses she shook her head.

'No.'

'So what exactly *did* you find out, Amelia?' Paul clipped, with no smile to follow, no small talk to pad it out—it was a direct question that needed a direct answer.

'That he looks beautiful asleep.' Her voice was a pale whisper and she screwed her eyes closed. 'You see, he was asleep when I got there…'

'So?' Paul thumped the desk. 'You make the guy a coffee, wake him with a bright smile…'

If only…

She couldn't look at him. Instead she stared at the card in her hand, listening as Paul took her on a virtual tour of a hundred ways to butter up a reluctant subject, his voice growing louder with each passing sentence. He was oblivious to the sudden shift in Amelia, totally unaware of the metamorphosis taking place before him, blind to the fact that the world had just tipped on its axis, that Christmas had come eleven months early, that Amelia was actually smiling—really smiling—back at him.

'What did you get from him, Amelia?' Paul's voice

was deadly serious, and at any other moment in time it would have had her shrinking in her seat.

'Nothing,' she said again, only more firmly this time, her smile still in place, enjoying for a luxurious moment the confusion in his eyes. 'He's picking me up here in an hour. We're going for dinner.'

'Vaughan Mason's taking you for dinner?' He didn't even attempt to hide the incredulity from his voice. 'Vaughan Mason?'

'At seven,' Amelia confirmed. 'As I said, he was too tired to do the interview.'

'Oh, my…' Paul was on his feet now, pacing the office floor, staring at Amelia with undisguised and unprecedented admiration. 'I told Clara you could pull it off.' He waved his finger at Amelia. 'She said you should have got changed before you went over, but I told her you'd win him over…'

'You did no such thing, Paul.'

Confidence suited her, Amelia realised, standing up and picking up the bouquet, burying her burning cheeks in the cool waxy petals and inhaling deeply. The scent that had been so oppressive was truly beautiful now. She was scarcely able to comprehend that Vaughan Mason had sent it to her—and in record time too—scarcely able to believe that these gorgeous, tropical flowers had somehow beaten her back to work and saved her in the very nick of time.

'I'd better get ready.'

'Good idea.' Paul jumped up. 'I'll ring one of the boutiques and ask them to stay open for you. And I can call Shelly the make-up artist to come and work her magic—'

'I've got an outfit in my locker,' Amelia interrupted, but Paul shook his head.

'This isn't one of your usual extended celebrity lunches; one of your little dark suits won't do here, Amelia. This is *dinner* with Vaughan Mason!'

Which did nothing to quell her nerves!

'I've actually got a gorgeous black dress in my locker,' Amelia said airily, not adding that she'd had it hanging there for six months now, draped in plastic, waiting for this moment—waiting for the big break to come—so she could dash like Wonder Woman into the office loo and change from efficient to gorgeous. 'But if Shelly's available that would be great.'

Poor Shelly. Amelia smiled as she sank back in a chair and closed her eyes—summoned from the bowels of the car park as she attempted to creep out to the pub on a Friday with the rest of the mob. Called back in to work her magic on someone who wasn't even famous—yet!

Gorgeous!

Okay, the dusty mirrors in the toilet had the same positive effect as a soft focus lens, but Shelly really was a genius. She'd been working on Amelia for forty full minutes, telling her sharply to stay still as Amelia had begged her to go lightly, sure she must look more like Coco the Clown from the amount of jars and tubes Shelly seemed to be opening. But now, staring back at her reflection, Amelia felt more than a flutter of excitement.

Cheekbones Amelia hadn't known existed made her look positively gaunt, and her mouth looked all sparkly and animated, courtesy of the very latest in 'stay put' lipglosses. But it was on her eyes where Shelly had really come into her own. A smudgy grey eyeshadow, that Amelia would never have attempted made the green so much more vivid, like glittering emeralds, her eyelashes impossibly long, and yet somehow she'd made it look if not subtle then tasteful. And as she stood and admired her reflection Amelia was scarcely able to believe that the sophisticated, demure woman staring back was really her.

'Oh, my,' Paul said for the hundredth time, barely able to contain his excitement as he stood waiting with her in the lobby. 'You've got spare batteries for your Dictaphone? Remember to turn off your mobile. There can be no distractions—not even from me. But if you need to call…'

'I'll be fine, Paul,' Amelia snapped, wishing he would just be quiet, wishing he would stop acting like some over-protective parent on his daughter's first date. 'Might I remind you, this isn't the first celebrity I've interviewed? I've delivered an article every week for the last six months.'

'But not one like this, Amelia.' Paul gave her an extremely annoying nudge as a slick silver car pulled up beside the pavement. 'This has shades of Taylor Dean written all over it—and look how much the paper made on that one article! Didn't he wrap up the interview by asking you to dinner?'

'This is nothing like Taylor Dean,' Amelia bristled, managing to simultaneously smile and give a small wave as she hissed the words out of the side of her mouth.

'No,' Paul responded. 'Because Vaughan Mason's got style.'

It was Vaughan who stepped out of the car, not his chauffer. Vaughan who pulled open the rear door as Paul walked down the concrete stairs with her and delivered his final below-the-belt remark.

'If you two aren't in bed by eleven, I want you to ring me at twelve.'

Amelia was used to heads turning as she made her way into restaurants, used to the nudges and murmurs working their way around the room like a game of Chinese Whispers as the patrons recognised her companion, and she was used to the best, most secluded table being somehow magically conjured up, whether or not a reservation had been made. But walking in with Vaughan she felt like a complete novice, a pit of nervousness in her stomach as his warm hand grazed the small of her back, guiding her through the white-clothed tables.

The glow on her cheeks was nothing to do with Shelly's generous rouge and everything to do with her delicious companion. Even her breathing wasn't involuntary as the waiter pulled out her chair and she took a grateful seat; every breath was a supreme effort as finally she faced him, as the moment it seemed she had been dreaming of all her life finally arrived.

'Why?'

It was the first real question that had spilled out of her lips, although they'd chatted politely in the back of his sleek car while his chauffer had driven them to this exclusive little French restaurant nestled in The Rocks.

Vaughan had declined an entrée, but, determined to wring the evening for every last drop, Amelia had ordered one. Even if it killed her she'd have dessert, and then port and cheese as well. She had the middle pages to fill!

Cracking the crust of her bread over her French onion soup, avoiding his eyes, Amelia found the nerve to ask the question that had been plaguing her since Paul's last derogatory remark. Despite the sheer heady pleasure of a night in Vaughan's company, she was utterly determined to set the tone early—to ensure Vaughan Mason understood that this was a business dinner and nothing else. Even if she might be merely flattering herself, Amelia had to be sure he had asked her here tonight for professional rather than personal reasons.

'Why the flowers? Why…?'

'Because on a last-minute impulse I picked up a bunch of orchids at Singapore Airport with the intention to give them to Katy as thanks for all her hard work. She's my PA,' he added, when Amelia frowned at his response. 'Anyway, suffice to say things became rather complicated, about ten minutes before you arrived in my office, and I'm sure that had I given the bouquet to Katy my life would have then taken a turn from complicated to extremely messy.'

'I meant why did you ask me for dinner?' Amelia asked, sure he had deliberately misinterpreted her question, but equally determined to get her answer.

'You asked about the flowers,' Vaughan pointed

out. 'It seemed a shame to waste them, so I asked Gary, my driver...' He relented with a devastating smile. Perfect white teeth lit up his dark features, brooding eyes holding hers over the table. 'I don't know why I asked you to dinner,' Vaughan admitted, taking a long sip of his whisky. 'I suppose I wanted to get to know you a bit better.'

'It's supposed to be the other way around, Mr Mason,' Amelia answered quickly.

His response was the last thing she needed, because it would be easy—so very frighteningly easy—to forget her promise to herself that she would never cross the professional line again! Even though there was no denying the attraction that sizzled between them, Amelia knew that if she weakened even for a moment, if she allowed herself to lapse for even a smidgen of time, Vaughan Mason would crush her in the palm of his manicured, experienced hand—use her and toss her aside, just as he had every woman who had come before her.

She had to stay in control.

'You couldn't get me out of your office quickly enough,' Amelia deliberately reminded him, 'so why the sudden change of heart?'

She watched him toying with the rim of his glass, stifling a yawn, but in a sharp contrast to their initial meeting his distraction didn't irritate her now. Something akin to compassion washed over her as she closely studied his face, took in the lines of exhaustion grooved around the edges of his eyes. The artist waiting in the wings must have left for an extended coffee break, because he'd forgotten to blend in those dark smudges beneath them. Vaughan was almost cross-eyed as he squinted across the table at her, and suddenly the hows and whys didn't matter any more; the fact she was here was quite simply enough.

'You're exhausted, aren't you?'

'Unfortunately, no.' He took another slug of his whisky. 'I was exhausted at five, and had you not burst into my office I suspect I'd still be lying on the sofa fast asleep. However...' he smiled at her darkening cheeks '...now I'm wide awake, and no doubt will remain that way until five a.m. tomorrow.'

'You're an insomniac.' Amelia groaned sympathetically. 'I used to be one too.'

'Don't.' He held up a beautifully manicured hand. 'Please don't try and engage me with your sympathy, telling me you understand exactly how I feel and then wiping the floor with me in the colour supplement.'

'You should try counting sheep.' A cheeky smile inched over her lips and she barely noticed the waiter delivering her sumptuous main course and tucking a massive white napkin around her. Amelia's eyes were only for her most intriguing subject.

'Which would no doubt be relaxing if I hadn't grown up on a massive sheep farm. I can still remember listening to thousands of them bleating as I tried to nod off.' He smiled at her open mouth. 'Don't you do *any* research, Miss Jacobs?'

'But nothing, *nothing* in your bio even hints that you grew up on a sheep farm. I thought that you went to an exclusive private school...'

'I did.'

'I specifically remember reading that your father is an accomplished businessman.'

'He is.'

Finally he relented.

'My father is an extremely successful sheep farmer.'

'Oh!' Pulling back, trying to quell the surprise in her voice, Amelia asked a more relevant question. 'Whereabouts?'

Vaughan immediately shook his head. 'That's hardly relevant.'

'I'm just interested,' Amelia responded, making a mental note to research it. But Vaughan was clearly a mind-reader.

'Don't even think about looking it up, Amelia. You can say what you like about me, but my family stays out of anything that you write.'

'I was hardly going to dig up dirt on him,' Amelia countered, but Vaughan remained unmoved.

'My family stays out of it,' he said again, very firmly and very clearly. 'The last thing I want is a picture of my father in his work gear, drinking his cup of tea out of the blessed tin mug he insists on using, and the papers bleating about how I keep them in rags. My father would be devastated. And before you say I'm overreacting, that you have no intention of writing such a piece, you might not, but some other journalist certainly will. You'd be amazed how things can get distorted.'

Amelia sighed. 'I wouldn't. Okay,' she conceded, 'family stays out of it—for the article at least. But can you tell me anyway?'

'Why do you want to know if you're not going to use it?'

Which was a good question, and one Amelia struggled for a short while to answer. Truth be known, she wanted to know only for herself—wanted to get to know the man behind the legend, dig just a little bit deeper for her own selfish reasons—but she could hardly tell him that. Instead she gave a small shrug.

'It just helps with my writing. The more I know about you, the more intimate the piece.'

'Oh, well, I'm all for intimate.' He gave a smile. 'My family has a large property in the Blue Mountains. So you see, counting sheep for me really isn't a relaxing option, given that come shearing time there are thirty thousand sheep to muster and shear over a four-week period. It's actually the stuff of nightmares, although I love doing it.'

'You still work the farm?'

'Absolutely. Like I said, there's only a small window of time to get the sheep sheared, and Dad's one rule is that we all head over there once a year for a fortnight to help out. I wouldn't miss it for the world.'

She was assailed with a vision of him in jeans and outdoor boots, that jet-black hair whipped up by the wind, a contrast to the sharp-suited immaculate man sitting before her. Amelia was having serious trouble deciding which one she'd prefer, knowing only one thing—she wanted to see them both.

'"We all"?'

'You don't miss a trick do you? My brother and I.'

'And does this brother of yours have a name?' She

watched him stiffen, but chose to pursue. 'Does this brother of yours have a family of his own?'

He wanted to tell her.

The internal admission startled him.

He wanted to tell this talkative, nosy woman about his mother and father, about his brother and his wife, about the child they both adored—wanted to share with her the inspiring beauty of the Blue Mountains he still called home: the damp, muggy smell of the fog as dawn crept in, the sweet taste of tea around a campfire, how, after a day of mustering, using his body instead of his brain, sleep for once came easily...

'Does your brother have children?' Her persistence was her downfall. The intrusion of another question snapped him back to reality, reminding him that this was a journalist sitting opposite him, and the words that had been on the tip of his tongue were swallowed along with a hefty belt of whisky.

'Like I said.' Vaughan gave a tight shrug. 'Family stays out of it.'

'Okay.' Clearly used to closed subjects, Amelia admitted defeat, shifting the topic to what she hoped was safer ground. 'How about reading?'

'Reading?'

'In bed.' Amelia grinned, but it wobbled midway. She was sure that Vaughan usually had far better things to keep him occupied in the bedroom, but she recovered quickly, pushing her line of questioning in the frantic hope of getting this very difficult man to open up a touch. 'To help you sleep—what sort of books do you like?'

'Crime novels. But the trouble with them is that I've no patience. I have to find out the end, which means…'

'You're up all night trying to finish it?' Amelia groaned in sympathy. 'I'm the same. What about something lighter—romance?' she teased, unable to fathom the sight of Vaughan lying in bed reading a love story. But to her utter surprise he nodded solemnly.

'Same problem. I'm up all night making sure they get together in the end. I'm a hopeless case, I'm afraid. Okay, funtime over.' He flashed a devilish smile. 'Let's get this over with—ask whatever it is you have to.'

'I don't work like that.' Amelia shook her head. 'Not when I'm doing an in-depth piece.'

Vaughan shuddered. 'Why don't I like the sound of that?'

'I find out a lot more just by talking…'

'You're certainly very good at that.'

'If you'd let me finish—' Amelia grinned '—I was about to say by talking with my subject in a relaxed setting—getting to really know them, finding out what's going on in their lives, building up a picture in my mind. It allows for a far more intimate portrayal than shooting a list of questions at them; anyone can do that. So the fun can continue.'

'And in the meantime is your *subject* allowed to get to know you?'

Her spoon paused midway from her plate.

'Of course.' Amelia recovered quickly. 'It's hardly

fair to expect someone to open up if I don't give a piece of me back.'

'So I can ask questions too?'

Amelia nodded, bypassing her champagne glass and reaching instead for a heavy glass of iced water. Her throat was impossibly dry all of a sudden, as she wondered what Vaughan Mason could possibly want to know about little old her.

'Did you tell your boss what I said about the motor deal?'

Not by a flicker did she express her disappointment; of course that was all he wanted to know—work was his bible, at least where a nosy journalist was concerned. As if he had been going to ask if she was single, Amelia mentally scolded herself. As if he were remotely interested in the woman sitting before him. And, more to the point, this was, at her insistence, strictly business.

'No.' Thankfully she was able to look him in the eye.

'Good.' Vaughan nodded. 'I don't believe in celebrating until I've got a signature on paper.' Watching her slender hands lift a fork that looked way too heavy to her mouth, Vaughan paused. Amelia's eyes closed in bliss as she sampled her food. 'Nice?'

'Fabulous.' Amelia sighed. 'Eating out is one of the serious perks of the job. I absolutely love my food.'

'Me too.' He smiled at her questioning eyebrow as she eyed the rather sparse plate the waiter was placing before him. The tomato salad with balsamic dressing he had ordered as a main course was clearly in sharp contradiction to his statement. 'Oh, no you don't. Before you label me as some temperamental bulimic…'

'I wasn't about to.' Amelia grinned.

'Oh, yes, you were. The fact is, I've had about ten meals today—a sumptuous breakfast in Japan followed by a large business lunch, then a three-course meal on the plane to Singapore, and to top that off another breakfast…'

'Okay, okay.' Amelia laughed, putting her hand up in mock defence. 'I get the message.'

'So you see there's a very good reason for a plain tomato salad…'

'You've got me all wrong.' Amelia was still laughing as she took a sip of her mineral water. 'I'm not interested in starting rumours, Mr Mason, just squashing them or confirming them. I'm as bored as most people with stories that have little foundation. I'm tired of ''confirmed'' pregnancies that never seem to get past the first trimester, or reading about an idyllic marriage only to turn on the news two weeks later and find out they're filing for divorce.'

Signalling the waiter, Vaughan sat back as Amelia's glass was refilled with the most expensive of champagnes and her slightly trembling hand toasted her most unexpected host.

'I like your work, Amelia.' It was the first time he'd called her by her first name, and it sounded more intimate than she'd ever heard it before. Vaughan Mason seemed to register that fact.

'Vaughan,' he affirmed, without suggestion. 'I

think we're both adult enough to deal with first-name terms.'

'You've read my work?'

He nodded. 'Every week, Amelia. And I don't know how you do it, but I have to hand it to you—somehow you manage to get the most unlikely of people to open up. Somehow you manage to slip in the most salacious piece of gossip and make it sound like girly talk. I have to admit it's making me a touch nervous.'

'You don't look it,' Amelia said, knowing he didn't mean it, but embarrassed and pleased all the same.

'So, how do you do it?'

'Do what?'

'Get them to open up?'

'I talk to them,' Amelia said simply. 'And, as for salacious gossip, I don't touch anything that hasn't already been hinted at. I see it as my job to give people the opportunity to confirm or deny. Which, so far, they have.'

'I'll say,' Vaughan responded, and Amelia felt her toes curl in pleasure at the dash of admiration in his voice. But her pleasure faded as Vaughan brought up the one name she really didn't want to hear ever again. 'That piece you did a few months ago where you got that alcoholic popstar to admit he'd been in rehab—you know the one…' He snapped his fingers, trying to recall the name, frowning as Amelia rather reluctantly filled him in.

'Taylor Dean.'

'That's the one.' Vaughan nodded. 'You didn't just get him to admit to being an alcoholic, you actually had him talking about how he'd dried out. How hellish the twelve steps had been for him. How? How did you get *him* to talk?'

'I asked him about it.' Amelia shrugged. 'Most people respond to a direct question. Most people, if they can see you're genuinely interested, are only too pleased to talk about themselves... Unlike you,' she added with a swift baleful look that was met with a smile. 'And, for the record, Taylor's a *recovering* alcoholic. He hasn't touched a drop for two years—at least that was the case when I wrote the piece.'

Vaughan didn't look particularly convinced, but Amelia refused to be drawn, instead fiddling with her glass and willing this part of the conversation to be over.

Thankfully Vaughan must have sensed her reluctance, because he swiftly moved on. 'How about that actress then? Miranda? For years I've wondered if she's had surgery, for years people have died wondering if she's been under the knife, and then you come along and suddenly we find out she's had the lot...'

'You really have done your research on me,' Amelia remarked, unable to keep the surprise out of her voice and suffused with both embarrassment and pride that this man had actually read her work—not just read it, but apparently enjoyed it.

'You're looking at a guy who spends half his life in airport terminals, Amelia. I read you because I like you.'

Maybe he was merely playing her at her own game—plying her with flattery—but here and now

Amelia didn't care. Because whatever Vaughan was up to, it felt good. His positive words were like a salve to her fragile ego, and she decided at that point to relish the moment instead of analysing it—there would be plenty of time for that when this magical night was over.

But Vaughan hadn't finished yet. He was pulling apart a bread roll and soaking up the last of his balsamic dressing—long fingers working the plate, a decadent flash of gold on his wrist. Even his hands were beautiful!

'As bitchy as your pieces are,' Vaughan carried on, his mouth full, but still looking impossibly sexy, 'they still come across as if you like your subjects.'

'Because I do like them—neuroses and all.' She smiled at his frown. 'I truly admire them.'

'Admire them?' Vaughan questioned. 'It hardly takes a degree in rocket science to croon into a microphone or to strut one's stuff on the catwalk. I've dated a few models in my time,' he added.

'I heard,' Amelia answered cheekily, before responding to his question. 'Okay, I admit at first I was a mixture of cynical and overawed. Yet the more I interview these people, the more I get to know them as individuals, and the more highly I think of them. Models deserve every last cent of their millions! Can you imagine sitting in a restaurant as divine as this and ordering a tomato salad with dressing on the side if you hadn't eaten ten courses today?' Her voice was truly appalled. 'Heaven knows—someone who can give birth and then get out of her hospital bed and do two hours of Pilates with only an egg-white omelette to look forward to is a woman who knows what she wants. I absolutely couldn't do it, and I tell them that.'

Her plate was being cleared away now. She ached to dash to the loo, to check that no remnants of food were between her teeth and that Shelly's make-up was living up to its reputation, but Vaughan was staring at her—staring across the table in a broody, pensive way. And if four years at uni had taught her anything it was that now was not the time to go, that if she left now, then a few minutes after returning so would he.

'My turn now,' Amelia said, and she took a deep breath, eternally grateful that she had a completely legitimate reason to ask the one question she really wanted answered; after all, not a woman in Australia would forgive her if she didn't find out his romantic status.

'Are you involved in a relationship?'

'I assume we're not talking about my family here? Because I am involved with them—very much so.'

'You assume correctly. So, are you involved with a woman?'

'Amelia!' Vaughan feigned surprise. 'I would have thought someone with your rather cosmopolitan job would phrase her questions more carefully—cast a wider net, perhaps. For all you know I could be gay.'

'Most gay men don't have your reputation with women, Vaughan,' Amelia answered with the sweetest of smiles.

'Ah, but how do you know that isn't just a smoke-screen?'

'Please!' Amelia scoffed, leaning back in her seat. And she would have laughed, was about to respond with some swift but witty retort, but both her laughter and her words died on her lips as she caught his eye. She stared at him for a full moment, meeting his gaze and holding it, and the background noise of the restaurant faded into silence. The moment dragged dangerously on, tipping her from unchartered to dangerous territory.

She didn't need to ask him. Not for a second had his being gay even entered her head—because Vaughan Mason, in the few hours since she'd known him, had made her feel more of a woman than she'd ever felt in her life.

'I think we both know that's not the case.' Her voice was amazingly even, given her accelerated heart-rate, but she wished he'd drop his gaze first—wished she could win this tiny unspoken battle. Whatever game they were playing, it didn't come with a rule book. His eyes were holding hers unblinkingly as she wrestled to come up with a response. 'However, I stand corrected. If you don't mind, I'll rephrase my question—are you in a romantic relationship?'

'No.'

The heady relief that flooded her shocked even Amelia, but determinedly she kept her features impassive, staring back at him, terrified to blink, to break the decadent beat of the moment. But this was work, Amelia reminded herself sharply. This was her career, the break she'd been praying for, and succumbing to Vaughan Mason's undeniable charms wasn't going to get her article written.

With a blinding flash of clarity she realised he was

playing her—playing her as he did every woman who had crossed his path for the last quarter of a century, playing her just as Taylor had.

These were men who had learnt to flirt from the cradle.

It was Amelia who dropped her eyes, Amelia who gave up on the game she could never win. Sitting up a notch and clearing her throat, she spoke in what she hoped was a more assertive tone than the rather more seductive one that seemed to have been waiting in the wings for the best part of the main course.

'You're thirty-four, Vaughan.'

'Thirty-five, actually.' He flashed a perfect white smile and Amelia was sure she could see a glint of triumph in his eye…

She knew that he knew that he'd moved her.

'Thirty-five,' Amelia corrected herself. 'Have you ever thought of settling down?'

'Settling down?' He frowned.

A tiny cough, a tiny reminder to herself that she was allowed to ask this type of question—it was her job to be nosy!

'Getting married?' Amelia responded through slightly gritted teeth, knowing he was merely stalling, dragging things out so he could prepare his answer.

'I've never understood that.' Vaughan frowned across the table. 'Why do people refer to marriage as ''settling down''? One would assume that you'd love the person you marry, yes?'

'One would hope so.' Amelia flashed a tight smile.

'And one could also assume, then, that you'd find that person incredibly sexually attractive. I mean, to actually have committed to that person for life you'd surely be sexually compatible, barely able to keep your hands off each other...'

Lucky, lucky woman, Amelia thought reluctantly. Lucky the woman who was the sole object of Vaughan Mason's desire, who had a man as utterly sexy as Vaughan permanently unable to keep his hands off her.

Trying to keep her breathing even, to keep a vaguely detached stance, she gave what she hoped was a vague nod, as if the picture he was painting in her mind *wasn't* causing her toes to curl under the table.

'Which hardly equates to settling down. Personally I'd refer to it as things hotting up—and considerably so.' He flashed a slightly triumphant smile. 'Does that answer your question?'

'Not in the slightest,' Amelia retorted, cheeks flaming, dying of embarrassment, but determined to get an answer. 'You do have a reputation,' she pointed out, then softened it with a smile. 'It would be almost criminally negligent not to broach the subject; my readers would never forgive me. You've been playing the field for quite some time, Vaughan.'

'But I've been sitting on the bench for a while. I *have*,' he insisted as Amelia's lips duly pursed. 'Leopards can change their spots, Amelia.'

'Or they learn to be more discreet,' Amelia responded dryly. 'Come on, Vaughan. I've heard it all before—same tune, different song...'

For a second his eyes narrowed, but then surprisingly he laughed. 'Where did a sweet thing like you learn to be so cynical?'

'It comes with the job description.' Amelia smiled back. 'I'm writing an article, not a fairy tale.'

'Taylor Dean changed,' Vaughan pointed out. 'You just said so yourself!' He registered the tiny swallow in her throat, the nervous dart of her eyes—read her as he read every woman who sat before him. 'You say the guy hasn't touched a drop in two years, yet every time he snaps at a shop assistant, every time he rocks up ten minutes late or cancels a gig because he has laryngitis, we're led to believe by your mob that he's back on the bottle. The guy can't cross the street without looking twice; the next thing he knows he's tomorrow's headlines...'

'Leave Taylor out of this.' Her voice was too shrill, too urgent, and Amelia fought to correct it, wishing somehow they could turn back the clock, revert to what they'd almost shared just a matter of seconds ago. 'We're talking about you...'

'I'm merely drawing an analogy. Anyway...' he frowned '...what happened between you two? How come you're so defensive...?'

He watched her flinch as if she'd been slapped, saw the colour literally drain out of her cheeks, her shaking hands reaching for her water glass. Normally it would have given him a kick, a tiny surge of thrill to have nailed it, to have hit the Achilles' heel that every living mortal had. Only this time it didn't. Watching her flounder, that effusive, expressive face struggling to remain bland, he instantly regretted the pain he'd inflicted, and took no pleasure in watching her flail. 'I'm sorry. That was way too personal.'

She forced a smile. 'If I can give it, I should be able to take it.'

'It's not always that easy, though, is it?' Vaughan suggested, gently now. 'We all make mistakes. Only most people don't have to get up in the morning and read about them. Most people can hide under the duvet for a few days and that's the end of it.'

Reaching in his pocket, he pulled out his mobile and frowned. 'I'd have thought Mr Cheng would have rung by now.'

Eternally grateful for the change of subject, she smiled more naturally.

'Maybe no news is good news?'

'Let's hope so.'

'When will you know for sure?'

'Next week. Mr Cheng is flying into Melbourne to check over a few last-minute details, and hopefully on Friday it will be in the bag. I should be able to announce it the following Monday. Thanks for not saying anything, by the way.'

'You said it was off the record.'

'Which normally means zilch.'

He watched her tongue bob out to lick her lips as the waiter placed her dessert in front of her. Integrity was seemingly ingrained in every one of her pores. Off the record for once meant just that.

'The Japanese company I am dealing with are shrewd businessmen. They're also incredibly well-mannered,' Vaughan explained, 'and more than a touch superstitious; blasting the story over the papers without Mr Cheng being informed would have been disastrous for progress. I'd have hated to face him on Monday if this had got out.'

Amelia nodded, sinking her spoon into the most delectable white chocolate and nougat mousse, knowing it was going to taste even better than it looked. The thought was confirmed as the sweet goo melted on her tongue.

'Nice?'

'Heaven,' Amelia sighed, taking another spoonful. 'I don't care how many meals you've eaten today, there's surely a pocket of space for this. You really don't know what you're missing.'

As innocent as a child, she held out the spoon for him to taste. Shaking his head, he stared into that elfin face. Her mascara had long since smudged, the lip-gloss had been lost somewhere between the main course and dessert, and Vaughan couldn't have disagreed with her more—he knew *exactly* what he was missing.

'Come.'

If her teeth hadn't been bound by nougat Amelia would have said something stupid, like *Where?* But the chocolate gods were being kind, allowing a semblance of sophistication as she refilled her water glass and washed down her dessert, forcing Vaughan to elaborate.

'Come to Melbourne with me next week.'

'Why?'

Even after a suitable pause, it wasn't the most sophisticated of answers. A *real* journalist would have murmured *I'd love to*; a real journalist wouldn't make her subject justify handing over such a magnificent scoop. But half a glass of champagne and a couple of hours in this divine man's company had eroded every last shred of sensibility.

'Well, if you're going to do an in-depth piece on me you might as well get the full picture. Of course there will be a few exceptions—I can't guarantee all of my contacts will want a journalist in the board-room, and I'd like to go to the pool unaccompanied in the morning, given that I can't swim and talk at the same time.'

'You swim?'

'I do.' Vaughan grinned. 'And, yes, you can use that. But, on a rather more serious note, one of the reasons I'm trusting you to do this piece is the un-believable fact that I haven't got fifty calls in my mes-sage bank asking me to confirm the motor deal.'

'I passed, then?'

'I guess so.' Vaughan smiled. 'But these are a cou-ple of ground rules. I don't mind you doing an in-depth piece on me, but my clients' names stay out of it.'

'Of course.' Amelia nodded.

'And, apart from my morning swim, I do have a personal life. Every now and then I will have to dis-appear.'

It came as no surprise to Amelia how much that piece of news depressed her, but she gave a solemn nod. And even if Paul might kill her, even if she was putting doubts into Vaughan's jet-lagged mind, Amelia couldn't refrain from pushing the point that she'd let go earlier.

'Why now, Vaughan? You've never given a personal interview, never allowed anyone to get close till now. What's caused the change of heart?'

'My advisors.' Vaughan rolled his eyes. 'Which sounds horribly affected, but no CEO worth his salt is without them these days and, given what I pay them, I guess I should try acting on some of the advice they so gleefully dish out. We both know that when—or rather at this stage *if* the motor deal's announced I'll be a hero. A hero next Friday but a villain by Monday.'

Sad, but true.

'Once the euphoria has worn off my rescue plan will be analysed and scrutinised…'

'And criticised,' Amelia offered, and Vaughan nodded.

'Jobs are going to go. The fact that without me within a year *every* job would have gone will be conveniently forgotten.'

'I thought you'd be used to being the bad guy by now.'

'I am.' Vaughan shrugged. 'But the fact of the matter is the press are going to go to town on this one.'

'I'm the press, Vaughan,' Amelia pointed out. 'Why do you think you'll get anything different from me?'

'I don't know,' Vaughan replied, but his confident expression belied the ambiguity of his words, and not for the first time Amelia had the feeling he was playing her.

'You can buy me all the white chocolate nougat I can stomach, tell me I'm the best journalist in Australia and massage my ego for hours, but I write the truth, Vaughan. You won't sway me for a moment.'

'I wouldn't dream of trying. And, no, I'm actually not asking you along to do a hearts-and-flowers piece on me. The truth would be refreshing enough!'

Amelia stared at him thoughtfully for a moment. His answer had almost convinced her, but there was one thing she needed to get out of the way—one thing she needed confirmed before she accepted the assignment. And if it sounded presumptuous, then so be it. There was no denying the sexual sparks cracking in the air around them, and to disregard them could only be to her detriment. By ignoring the sparks she could be fanning the flames, which was a dangerous game indeed—especially with such a skilful player as Vaughan.

'Would you have asked Carter?'

'Carter's after a different angle. His mind's stuck purely on business.'

'So is mine,' Amelia retorted sharply, but Vaughan just laughed.

'I was actually referring to the different section of the newspaper that Carter covers. But if that's what's worrying you...'

'I'm not *worried*, Vaughan. I just like to make things clear from the outset.'

'Which you have,' Vaughan replied easily, smothering a yawn before signalling for the bill. 'And if it makes you feel any more comfortable I *never* mix business with pleasure—well, not recently anyway. It's a definite new rule of mine. It makes things far too messy and complicated. Katy today is a prime example. Believe me, Amelia, if I want casual sex I can think of easier ways of getting it than having a journalist glued to my side for a week.'

And therein lay the problem. With two small words he'd affirmed what she'd guessed.

Casual sex.

Walking out onto the street, momentarily blinded by the flash of photographers, Amelia managed a wry smile at their wasted efforts. Curses would later fill the darkrooms of rival newspapers as her face came into focus alongside Vaughan's, when they realised that not only did Vaughan Mason not have a hot date tonight, but she, Amelia Jacobs, had landed a wonderful scoop.

Refusing his offer of a lift, Amelia hailed a taxi, firmed up a time to meet him at the airport, then climbed into the back seat, managing a small wave as the taxi pulled off. But all the time her heart was hammering, her cheeks flaming at his throwaway comment.

Casual sex was all a man like Vaughan wanted from women, and she mustn't forget it—not even for a moment.

CHAPTER THREE

'NO PROBLEM getting away?' Vaughan greeted her, and Amelia gave a crisp smile.

'No problem,' she confirmed—which was the understatement of the year!

Paul had practically died on the spot in delight when she'd told him—in fact, she was surprised he wasn't here at the airport now, to wave her off, hiding behind a pot-plant and attempting to catch her alone so he could give her just one more piece of vital advice.

After she'd told her editor of Vaughan's invitation the whole weekend had been a blur of vital advice—the questions she should ask, the subjects she should avoid. The only time Paul had been silent was when Amelia had asked him about the big story the paper was due to break on Vaughan.

'Like I said, Amelia, it's best you don't know.'

'Best for who?' Amelia pushed. 'How can I do an informed piece when my own paper's holding back on vital information? If there's something about to go down with the motor deal, surely I should be aware—'

'It's nothing to do with the motor deal,' Paul broke in.

'Personal, then?' Watching Paul's eyes dart away a fraction too soon, Amelia knew she'd hit the nail on the head. 'Is he about to get engaged? Has he got some love-child…?'

'Stop fishing, Amelia. Just do your work and I'll do mine. I want your copy by two p.m. on Friday and not a second later. We're going to use it this same weekend. Not,' he added, with an utterly wasted reassuring smile, 'that I want you to feel as if you're under pressure.'

'Just know that I am,' Amelia retorted, relishing the task ahead yet terrified all of the same.

And now here she stood, in a boxy little suit, hair slicked back, and looking not too bad given she'd had approximately five minutes' sleep the entire weekend. Her luggage was checked in, the newspaper was under her arm, her boarding pass was in her hand, and Australia's most eligible bachelor was at her side.

Life was certainly looking up.

Better still if he whizzed her off to some scrummy first-class lounge for a decent cup of coffee to wake her up while they waited for their flight. But that hope was soon dashed when Vaughan told her that, given how she'd managed to get there on time, he'd checked them onto an earlier flight.

'I'm going to get something to read. Do you want anything?'

'No, thanks,' Amelia answered, tapping the newspaper under her arm.

'You're sure?' Vaughan checked, pulling a suitably bored face at her choice of in-flight entertainment.

'I like to keep abreast—anyway, you don't really have time to go to the newsagent's, Vaughan. The six-thirty's already boarding.'

'So?' he answered with annoying arrogance, striding off towards the newsagent's.

And because it was all business passengers, because there were no irate toddlers or wheelchairs to board, the line of red-eyed passengers filed in quickly—leaving Amelia standing alone, avoiding the eye of an irritated air stewardess, who was chatting into the wall phone and tapping on the computer, and wondering just what the hell was taking Vaughan so long.

'Miss Jackson?' the air stewardess called, replacing the phone's receiver. 'I'm going to have to ask you to board now, please. The door's about to close.'

'It's Miss *Jacobs*,' Amelia corrected, hoping she sounded assertive. 'I'm just waiting for my colleague. He shouldn't be too much longer.'

'Well, when he returns you can tell *your colleague* that he's just missed his flight,' the stewardess huffed, tapping into the computer with impossibly long nails. 'The gate has just closed. I'll see if there are any spaces on the seven a.m. What's your colleague's surname?'

'Mason,' Amelia answered, scanning the empty corridor, praying for him to appear, terrified the whole week ahead wasn't even going to get past the first hurdle. 'Vaughan Mason.'

It was like watching a soluble aspirin drop into a glass.

The pretty face, set in stone, suddenly fizzed into animated life. The impassive stance gave way and the air stewardess positively sparkled at the mere mention of his name. Gone was the bossy harridan tapping into the computer, instead she was actually moving—walking, in fact—over to the seriously camp air steward who was shooting daggers at Amelia as he appeared at the desk.

Make that two soluble aspirin, Amelia thought darkly as the air steward caught sight of his wayward passenger, carrier bag bulging, thumbing through a glossy magazine, not remotely in a hurry.

Vaughan made his way over.

'Mr Mason!' Amelia wasn't sure who said it first, both steward and stewardess were talking in effusive tones, practically carrying him along the carpeted walkway as Amelia padded behind. 'We didn't realise you were travelling with us this morning—what a pleasure.'

'What's wrong?' Vaughan asked as Amelia sat, still bristling, in her seat.

The plane taxied along the runway, and the sigh from the passengers was audible when the captain announced that they'd missed their slot and would have to wait another fifteen minutes before take-off.

'Nothing.' Amelia sniffed, and waited for him to push, to ask if she were sure, but when Vaughan merely dug into his carrier bag and pulled out another magazine Amelia chose to elaborate. 'If you'd been anyone else, the flight would have gone.'

'Probably,' Vaughan conceded.

'Yet you expected it to wait,' Amelia went on, warming to her subject. 'You kept a whole planeload of people sitting here while you chose a pile of magazines…' Anger mounting, she watched as he unwrapped a toffee and popped it into his mouth. 'And a load of sweets. Don't you think that's rather arrogant, Vaughan?'

'You clearly do!'

'Yes,' Amelia replied hotly, 'I really do. Now, I know I'm here merely to observe, but, given that you've involved me, I think I have a right to say something here!'

'Go ahead,' Vaughan offered, but he sounded so bored Amelia half expected him to put on the eyepads located in the little goody bag they had been handed.

'You change our flights because we're early, and then, instead of boarding at the correct time, instead of being pleased we'd been accommodated earlier, you head off to the newsagent, leaving me standing like an idiot to make excuses for your thoughtless behaviour.'

'Thoughtless?'

'Yes, thoughtless.' Her hand flailed, gesturing to the window, to the grey of the airport buildings as the plane taxied slowly along. 'Just so that you had something to read, you've ensured that two hundred people's schedules are put out for the day. I'd say that's pretty thoughtless Vaughan.'

'I guess it is,' Vaughan sighed. 'I just felt sorry for her.'

'For who?' Amelia frowned.

'The girl at the newsagent. It was only her second day, and she'd run out of till paper. I said I didn't want a receipt, but she insisted—said that she'd get into trouble if she didn't give me one.'

'Oh!' Blinking back at him, Amelia almost apologised, even opened her mouth to do so. But the ghost of a smile twitching at the edge of his lips gave him away, and her mouth snapped closed as she almost swallowed his bare-faced lie.

'Guess I'm just an arrogant bastard!' He winked, with no trace of an apology, and turned back to his magazine, laughing out loud at the problem page and then wincing loudly, not even bothering to flick over the page, from a before and after shot of breast enlargement surgery.

The air steward hovered to *double check* that his seatbelt was done up, and Amelia struggled through the business section of her paper, reading the most boring article about gender balance in the workplace and longing to bury herself in one of Vaughan's glossies.

But she'd die before asking.

'Help yourself,' Vaughan offered, as Amelia's eyes wandered for the third time in two minutes to the magazine he was holding. He held it out to her. 'I'm keeping *abreast* myself—though I have to admit it looks like bloody agony. Why do women do it?'

'That's a rather in-depth topic for six forty-five in the morning,' Amelia bristled, and Vaughan rolled his eyes.

'Just making small talk. Look…' his voice lowered '…this could end up being a very long week if we don't set a few ground rules: you want to see me warts and all; I want an honest piece written.'

'Yes,' Amelia agreed.

'So get your own back at the end of the week. Toss in a spiteful, cutting line about how thoughtless I am, if it makes you feel better, but please, don't sit next to me smarting. File it and save it for later.'

The rest of the flight was spent in rather more companionable silence. Amelia nibbled on a warm chocolate muffin, leafing through one of Vaughan's magazines, as he in turn drank three impossibly strong coffees and read, with markedly more interest than Amelia, the business section of her newspaper, barely even glancing up as the plane made its descent.

The hotel was as impossibly decadent. Vaughan glided through check-in as silent bellboys whizzed away their luggage, and with one glimpse of the massive bed as she stepped into her king-size suite, Amelia wanted to peel off her stilettos there and then and climb right in.

'All right?' Vaughan checked, knocking sharply on her door and not even waiting for a reply before he let himself in. 'I asked for adjoining rooms. I figured it would be easier to meet up that way.'

'It's fine,' Amelia replied nonchalantly, while privately imagining Paul's reaction when she put in her expense-claim form. 'Oh, look!' Peeling back the sheer curtains, she stared at the magnificent view below—there was not a glint of summer sky in sight; the entire complex faced in on itself, and the courtyard below was filled with early-morning Melburnians, pulling apart croissants and reading newspapers.

'That's a nice place to eat,' Vaughan said, nodding downwards to where a massive grand piano was the focal point of the dining area. 'Though I normally choose to eat on the balcony.' He gestured to the four square feet of space adjoining hers.

'We can wave to each other,' Amelia suggested, then, taking a deep breath, figured it was time to set *her* ground rules. 'Look, Vaughan, the last thing I want to do is crowd you. I'm thrilled you've entrusted me to do this piece, but if at any time over the next few days you need your space, then just say so.'

'Likewise,' Vaughan agreed, a flicker of relief washing over his face.

'So...' Amelia grinned as still he stood there.

'So?' Vaughan questioned.

'I'd like to unpack, and get better acquainted with that divine shower...' Her voice trailed off as Vaughan shook his head and glanced at his watch. 'Later?'

'Later.' Vaughan nodded. 'Much, much later.'

His staying power was formidable.

Even the chauffer-driven car constantly on call didn't suffice for his impossible schedule. Half an hour negotiating traffic was a sheer waste of Vaughan Mason's time, and if a helicopter ride across the city meant an extra few minutes could be crammed into his schedule, then that was the means of transport.

Amelia held her breath as she saw the Melbourne skyline from an entirely different angle, then barely had time to drag her fingers through her chopper-tousled hair before breezing into meeting upon meeting. She was completely aware that these meetings had been scheduled weeks if not months in advance, that a slice of Vaughan Mason's acumen was an expensive commodity, but over and over he delivered—commanding the entire room, ramming home his points. Most surprisingly of all for Amelia, she was allowed in to each one.

If Vaughan had okayed it then apparently it was fine…

'She's doing a piece on me,' Vaughan would shrug arrogantly. 'Not you, Marcus.' Or Heath, or any other poor soul whose business was being put through the shredder.

And she watched—watched the nervous, sweating faces around the boardroom tables as Vaughan, utterly composed, completely unmoved, sliced through their reams of excuses, their reasons, their attempts to justify the mess that had led them to this point, as easily as a hot knife through butter, cutting directly to the chase, exposing raw truths, absolutely ruthless in his assessments.

'Some of these staff have been with us for years!' Marcus Bates visibly reeled at the brutal proposal Vaughan had outlined, balking at the prospect of laying off so many staff. 'We can't just throw them onto the dole queue. Some of these people are in their fifties…'

'Which means they'll receive a decent pay-out,' Vaughan pointed out, his voice like ice, watching as Marcus took a shaky drink of the cup of coffee in front of him, staring him down, until Marcus finally admitted to his directors the absolute, unsavoury truth.

'We can't afford to pay anyone out,' he said, his

voice a hollow whisper, his shirt drenched in perspiration and his face like white putty.

Amelia actually felt sorry for this man she had never till now even met, as she glimpsed the impossible weight of the truth he had been carrying for months, perhaps even years, and the silence seemed to go on for ever.

'Finally,' Vaughan said slowly, 'we're getting to the truth. The fact is you can't even afford the coffee beans in your expensive machine.'

He stared around the table, stared at each nervous person in turn, and despite the smell of fear in the room Amelia could almost taste the respect as each pair of eyes looked to Vaughan for an answer, looked to the legend for a last-minute reprieve.

'The staff we lay off *will* be paid out,' Vaughan responded finally, and an audible sigh of relief went around the room as Vaughan Mason took on the impossible and the *you* became *we* as he flicked through the mountain of papers in front of him, hurling a chosen few across the table. 'And if that means you have to forgo your extended lunches and bring in your own cheese sandwiches for the next twelve months then it's a small price to pay, given the direness of your situation—these expense claims are deplorable! I want every member of staff entitled to a company car driving the same model and vehicle, at least while I'm running this ship. Believe me, guys, I want every last teabag accounted for in this place...'

Despite the brand-new stilettos which had rubbed the skin off the backs of her heels, and despite the utter exhaustion of the whirlwind that had blitzed her life seventy-two hours ago, over and over he impressed. Over and over she pressed the button on her digital Dictaphone to record a genius at work, even while knowing it was useless. Unless you were there, unless you actually witnessed him at first hand, holding the floor, utterly commanding, then it would take more than a degree in journalism to capture his formidable presence—the might that was Vaughan Mason could never be confined to a single article.

Yet she ached to try, her fingers literally itching to pound her keypad, to somehow get down the jumble of thoughts in her mind, and she was infinitely grateful for that fact as, for maybe the twentieth time that day, she found herself in the confined space of a lift with him. Only this time it was gliding them back up to their hotel rooms.

The hum of the lift was a blissful contrast to the lively chatter of the Japanese restaurant Vaughan had chosen for Mr Cheng, and Amelia was infinitely grateful for the fact that she could force her mind to focus on the work ahead and push aside the nerve-racking yet vaguely delicious feeling of claustrophobia that had seemed to hit her at various moments through the day, and was now peaking with alarming ferocity as the evening gave way to night.

'Interesting evening?' Vaughan asked, restless eyes scanning the lift numbers as he smothered a yawn.

'Very.' Amelia nodded. 'Especially the dessert.'

'I was talking about—'

'I know you were.' Amelia grinned. 'Actually, I'm still reeling from the fact that they all let me in. You'd hardly think a journalist would be permitted in some of those buildings, let alone in the meeting rooms. Look at Noble and Bates—I mean, I know there's been a few whispers, but why would they take the risk of allowing me in? Obviously I'm not going to name names, but why on earth would they allow a journalist in to hear that their business's back is against the wall.'

'But it isn't,' Vaughan answered as the lift door pinged open and they walked along the thickly carpeted corridor to their adjoining rooms. 'At least not any more.'

'You heard the figures, Vaughan!' Amelia responded, hobbling along on heels that were seriously killing her now, not quite comfortable enough to slip them off in his presence!

'I'm sure they're far worse!' Vaughan answered easily. They were at his door now, and she watched as he swiped his access card, pushing the door open and holding it that way with his wide shoulders. 'Look, Amelia, today had nothing to do with trust or risk, at least not on Noble and Bates's part. You're right—there have been whispers, and they're getting louder by the day and the directors know it. Their quarterly figures are about to be released and there are going to be a lot of shareholders baying for answers. Now they've got one.'

'What?'

'Me,' Vaughan answered without a trace of modesty, and somehow it suited him. 'I don't take on nohopers and everyone knows that.'

'But their figures are appalling,' Amelia answered,

genuinely confused. 'Do you really think they can recover?'

'My word, they're going to. Especially given the fact that for the next three years Noble and Bates will be paying me ten per cent of their profits—and, given that I intend to keep right on living well, I'm going to make damn sure they're healthy ones. My team and I will whip their sorry butts into shape, get rid of all the dead wool that's been holding them back, and everybody knows it.'

'Wood,' Amelia corrected. 'The dead wood.'

'Wool.' Vaughan gave a glimmer of a smile. 'Growing up on a sheep farm taught me a lot of things, and one of them is that underneath that tired-looking old sheep is a little lamb waiting to skip off— and I intend to expose it.'

And he would. Amelia didn't doubt it.

Confidence was contagious, and Vaughan Mason epitomised the word. The mere fact he was taking them on, the mere fact he was prepared to invest his time in the ailing company, would be more than enough to appease the shareholders.

He'd never been wrong.

Amelia's mind raced for one exception to the rule, but admitted defeat almost instantly.

'Lucky Noble and Bates, then.' Amelia smiled up at him, but it faded midway. Nothing, *nothing* in his stance had changed—his shoulder was still blocking the door, his face was exactly the same as the last time she had looked—yet *everything* had shifted. Business was clearly over; senses were trickling in. Shifting her weight on her tired aching feet, self-conscious under his scrutiny, her voice was slightly croaky as she wrapped up what she was saying. 'Having you to rescue them...'

Again she shifted her weight, and Vaughan gave her the gift of another small smile.

'New shoes?'

Amelia grimaced. 'They're too small. They didn't come in my size.'

'Then why on earth did you buy them?' Vaughan asked, clearly completely bemused.

'I guess I fell in love.' Amelia gave a tiny shrug. 'It was either these or go without completely.'

'And was it worth the pain?'

Amelia thought of her bruised, raw, shredded feet, but without hesitation nodded. 'Absolutely.'

For a beat he hesitated too, and Amelia was sure that for that fraction of time he was thinking about asking her in, weighing up in that calculated mind of his the pros and cons of prolonging this long day. And she only knew that she couldn't do it—couldn't enter into that room and hope to retain a distant façade.

'I'd better get on,' she attempted, as still he stared down. 'Paul will be screaming for my word-count.'

'Shame,' Vaughan said softly, but didn't elaborate, walking into his room without a backward glance.

The door closed gently behind him, leaving Amelia standing, mouthing like a goldfish at the smart mahogany woodwork, a retraction on the tip of her tongue, bitterly regretful that she hadn't said yes to his offer.

CHAPTER FOUR

'WELL?'

Somehow Paul managed to deliver twenty questions with a single word.

'I haven't actually written anything to send you yet,' Amelia started, thankful for the hands-free phone so she could pace the room, as she always did when she was nervous; talking to Paul always made her nervous. 'We've only just got in. But I've got lots of material.'

'Such as?'

'I'm not sure yet,' Amelia answered feebly. 'I'm still building a picture.'

'If I wanted photos I'd have sent a photographer along with you,' Paul retorted nastily. 'I want words, I want facts, and I want details...'

'Paul!' Halting his tirade, even Amelia was shocked at the force behind her own voice. 'This is my piece. *My* piece,' she added, more so she could affirm it to herself than to Paul—assertiveness not really her forte at the best of times. 'You'll get your words and I can assure you they'll be interesting—riveting in fact—but if you're hoping for me to do a hatchet job on Vaughan Mason then you're going to be sorely disappointed. If you want facts and details, then give me a permanent job in the business section of the paper instead of a painfully temporary freelance position in the colour supplement.'

'Do this right,' Paul responded, 'and you'll have your permanent job, Amelia. You know that as well as I do.'

Her lack of response spoke volumes.

'That *is* what you still want, I assume?'

Amelia didn't answer; she truly couldn't. She had suddenly realised that she didn't really know what she wanted any more—the dream she'd chased for so long was so close now she could almost reach out and touch it, so why was she stalling? Why was she closing her eyes and having second thoughts?

'Just deliver a good piece and then we'll talk about it,' Paul concluded. 'But in the meantime remember who's paying that over-inflated hotel bill.'

And she would, Amelia decided, pulling open her laptop and flicking it on. Now really wasn't the most convenient of times to be having a career crisis!

Locating the file she'd set aside for her article, Amelia fiddled with the margins for a full moment before attempting to start. Her fingers hovered over the keys for an inordinate amount of time, even though they'd been itching to get started before Paul's call had stifled them.

As good for her career as it might be, she didn't want to waste even a second of her word-count on Noble and Bates—there were hundreds of journalists who'd be only too willing to step in and do that when the time came. Instead she wanted—no, needed to somehow divulge to her readers the subject she was spending time with, to transport them on a bleary

Saturday morning to an alien world, to let them glimpse the man that was Vaughan Mason, allow them to glimpse the real person behind the hype…

To keep on doing what she had been for six months…

Wanted or not, a career crisis was exactly what she was having!

Pulling open the French windows, she let the clatter of diners below fill the room, pleasantly masked by the skilful fingers of a pianist. Stepping out onto the balcony she stared down, closing her eyes and letting the music soothe her, trying to put Paul's words out of her mind and focus on what it was she really wanted to do with her life.

'Problem?'

His voice was so close she literally jumped, turning, startled, to the balcony beside hers, where Vaughan sat nursing a huge brandy, totally relaxed in a massive toweling robe. His black hair was even blacker from the shower, and Amelia's body shot into overdrive. Even an intravenous shot of hormones couldn't have delivered a more potent effect. The mere sight of Vaughan away from the boardroom and in a clearly relaxed frame of mind was literally intoxicating. All she could manage was a feeble shake of her head.

'If you don't mind my saying, you look a bit anxious.'

She *felt* a bit anxious, but right now it had nothing to do with Paul and everything to do with the man on the next balcony.

The strategic waist-high Perspex wall between balconies was at least a semblance of a barrier, and it gave Amelia enough room to move mentally, feign nonchalance and give a small shrug.

'It's just a work issue.'

'So, tell me,' Vaughan offered, holding up the bottle, 'and on this side of the fence, preferably. I don't fancy shouting over Frank.'

As Amelia gave him a slightly perplexed look he added, 'Sinatra.' And a smile broke on her pale lips as, sure enough, the pianist broke into a musical rendition of a very old favourite. 'I've been here enough to know the pianist's routine by now. Come over and talk about it.'

'I'd say you're the last person I should be discussing my work problems with,' Amelia refuted, but of course Vaughan had an answer.

'On the contrary. I'm probably the *first* person you should be discussing them with, given that no doubt I'm the root of the problem.'

'That's very presumptuous.'

'But accurate,' Vaughan responded, at her darkening cheeks. 'Now, given that for the first time in living memory I'm offering some free advice, and given that however presumptuous it sounds I'm extremely good at what I do, then I'd take it if I were you.'

'It is about you,' Amelia admitted. 'Well, sort of. So how can I possibly…?'

'I can be very objective,' Vaughan persisted.

'I really need to have a shower,' Amelia attempted as a last line of defence, but Vaughan dealt with that excuse just as easily.

'It's way before my bedtime.' He flashed a wicked grin. 'Go and have your shower and I'll pour you a drink.'

Which sounded simple.

Which should be simple, Amelia thought, turning the knob in the shower and getting drenched in freezing water by a shower head that was surely as big as a dinner plate. But even a shower of icy water couldn't douse the nerves that were jumping now. And why, Amelia wondered, was she shaving her legs when she'd only done them last night? Why was she squeezing every last drop out of the tiny bottle of moisturising lotion the hotel provided and rubbing it into every inch of her body?

What should she wear?

The never-ending question that bypassed men and perpetually plagued women was making itself heard. Her entire suitcase was filled with smart business suits and endless strappy little numbers which she had packed for formal occasions. Sophisticated chic had been very much the order of the day when she'd been packing; tête-à-têtes in Vaughan's hotel room had definitely not been on the agenda. The only exception to the rule was a very skimpy pair of boxer shorts and a crop top that were strictly for bed.

Alone!

Punching in Vaughan's room number, she made one of the most embarrassing phone calls of her life.

'Would you believe me if I told you I have nothing to wear?'

'It's midnight, Amelia,' Vaughan drawled. 'We'll

be sitting on a balcony talking and drinking brandy. You hardly need to dress up for the occasion.'

'Exactly,' Amelia sighed. 'But according to my suitcase *dress up* is all I can manage. Had you been asking me to a ball I'd be appropriately dressed—stunning, actually. Coffee in Chapel Street—no problem at all. But casual…'

'Walk towards the bathroom Amelia.' She could feel his smile and it made her lips twitch too. 'Pull open the door and what do you see?'

'Deodorant, toothpaste…'

'Okay, close the door. Now what do you see?'

'A towelling robe,' Amelia wailed. 'But I can't come over dressed—'

'We'll be matching.' Vaughan grinned down the phone.

Even though she was draped from head to toe in inch-thick terry towelling fabric, even though not a glimpse of newly shaved, freshly moisturised flesh was on show, Amelia felt as naked and as exposed as if she were wearing only the bottom half of a bikini. Knocking on his door with a tentative hand, she wished she had her time over and had thought to rouge her cheeks or add a splash of lipgloss to her lips—even the dreadful jeans she had first greeted him in would be preferable to this!

Damn!

It was the only word that resounded in his mind as he opened the door.

Damn, damn, damn!

Straight back to go, straight back to the beginning

of the game, when she'd spun into his office, gamine, hair damp, large eyes glittering in her wary face. Straight back to where he'd completely dropped his guard.

Yet he'd seen more women dressed in exactly the same attire than he cared to remember, Vaughan reminded himself as he let her in. Had opened the door over and over to a terry towelling robe with a voluptuous woman inside—so why the panic now?

Because normally the heavy scent of perfume was the first thing to greet him, followed by tumbling hair and a well made-up face. Normally Vaughan knew exactly what was on the agenda, but the signs were completely unreadable here.

If Housekeeping had taken to installing buttons on the robes, then Amelia's were done up the neck. The lapels were pulled tightly, the belt firmly double-knotted around her waist, and she was even wearing the slippers the hotel provided, unpainted toes peeping out. If nothing else they were something for him to focus on as he beckoned her inside, trying to ignore the sweet scent of shampoo and toothpaste and completely nothing else. Her eyes were utterly devoid of make-up, her hair still wore the marks of the comb she must have raked through it, yet for all her complete lack of effort, for all her hidden womanly charms, she was, quite simply, the most delicious parcel of femininity he had ever seen.

As wary as a puppy being let inside for the first time, she stalked into the room, tail firmly between her legs, as if any moment now she expected to be shooed out. Yet despite the vulnerability and the absolute lack of warpaint, despite the almost child-like demeanour, Vaughan knew from the way his body responded that it was every inch a woman crossing his threshold tonight.

Amelia wasn't faring much better. Even though their rooms were identical, Vaughan had already stamped his identity on his—the lights were dimmer and the air, still damp from a no-doubt extended shower, was filled with his heavy cologne plus that unique masculine smell that had assailed her over and over in the lifts. Damp white towels littered the floor— Vaughan was clearly only too happy for someone else to pick them up—and his dresser was littered with his watch and heavy silver cufflinks, his wallet and mobile.

But far more intimidating than the dim lights and the heady scent of maleness was the wide-shouldered man walking in front of her towards the balcony. Even his back view was somehow effortlessly divine—superbly cut hair, for once wet and tousled, belt loosely knotted around snaky hips and a glimpse of toned muscular calves peeping out at the bottom.

She felt as if she were stepping inside somewhere decadent and forbidden, like a teenager entering a bar for the first time—painfully self-conscious, feeling as sophisticated as a gnat, almost waiting for a bouncer to appear, to tell her to leave, that she should never have been let in, that this was somewhere a woman like Amelia quite simply shouldn't be.

'Brandy?'

He hadn't poured it yet—they weren't even outside—but she could see a second glass waiting by the bottle on the balcony. Amelia shook her head, deciding her wits were firmly needed about her person. 'I'll just have a hot chocolate.'

'I'll ring down for Room Service.'

'Please don't.' Pulling open a cupboard Vaughan hadn't even known existed, she plugged in a tiny kettle, peeled open a sachet of powder and poured it into a mug, taking her time to make her brew before joining him outside.

'This is a terrible idea,' Amelia groaned, breaking the ice with her valid concerns. 'Despite what you say, I can hardly hope for objective advice. You don't even know what the problem is.'

'Don't tell me—let me guess.' Vaughan waited a moment till she'd sat down. 'The papers are asking for blood? ''Forget the intimate portrayal, Amelia, we know you can deliver on that. You've got Vaughan Mason to yourself for a week and we want you to give us the dirt—give us a story that's going to grab the headlines''.'

She didn't even feign surprise that he already knew, just nodded wearily.

'So why don't you? You know about the motor deal, you know about Noble and Bates—why don't you give the paper what they want and make a bigger name for yourself in the meantime? You said in my office that you desperately wanted to move into business reporting—well, here's your chance.'

For an age she thought, forming an answer she hadn't even properly run by herself.

'I don't know if it's what I really want to do any more, Vaughan.'

It sounded so straightforward, but as she tucked her legs under her, closing her eyes for a moment, he knew it was anything but.

'My father's a political reporter...'

'Grant Jacobs!' She watched as he made the connection. 'Now, that really is a hard act to follow—he's brilliant.'

'Brilliant,' Amelia sighed. 'My father is a *real* journalist—or so he keeps telling me. He dashes off at a moment's notice to some wartorn country, appears on horribly blotchy videophone news reports, talking about bombings and death and danger, and holds tiny famine-struck babies in his arms. For ages he hoped that I'd follow in his footsteps...'

'But it's not for you?'

'They haven't invented a waterproof mascara good enough yet,' Amelia admitted. 'Still, I've always liked journalism, I've always known that was what I wanted to do, and business was what always interested me. I was the nerdiest kid, Vaughan. I'd read my horoscope and then promptly turn to the business section to see what the US dollar was up to. Business has always fascinated me.'

'But?' he asked, because clearly there was one.

'When I took the job I'm doing now I saw it as a foot in the door with a major newsgroup—a step in the right direction, perhaps. Build up my portfolio a bit, make myself known.' She gave a wry smile. 'Pay off my car! But I never thought I'd end up loving it.'

'Which you do.' It was a statement not a question.

'Absolutely. My father winces every Saturday when he reads my pieces—says repeatedly that he can't believe that the daughter of a respected political correspondent could lower herself to write such trash.'

'I like it,' Vaughan ventured, and his small vote of praise was rewarded with a tired smile.

'So do I—and that's what's confusing me. I never intended for this to be permanent,' Amelia said, stirring her hot chocolate into a mini-whirlpool. 'When I was offered the weekly slot, naturally I was thrilled. But…'

'You had no intention of it lasting for ever?'

'None at all. It was only a maternity leave position. I actually wanted—'

'You don't have to justify your reasons to me,' Vaughan broke in, cutting to the chase in his usual analytical way. 'So what's changed in the last six months?'

'I like what I do.' For the first time since stepping onto the balcony she looked at him. 'In fact, I love what I do.'

'So where's the problem?'

She didn't answer—couldn't, really. But Vaughan did it for her.

'If you give them what they want now, then they'll make your position more permanent—maybe even move you to the business side of things?'

Her silence was his affirmation.

'Well, why don't you do it, Amelia? You've got more than enough to grab the headlines—surely this will open a few doors for you?'

'That wasn't the deal. This was never supposed to be a business piece—that's the reason you brought me along. It's hardly fair for me to change my mind midway.'

'It wouldn't be the first time I've been stitched up by a newspaper. I'm sure I'd survive—and I'm sure Noble and Bates would too. As I said before, they probably want the story to come out.' His eyes narrowed, staring at her thoughtfully for a long moment. 'Let's not kid ourselves that you're worried about protecting my feelings, that it's some ingrained integrity holding you back. We all know journalists don't have any.' He didn't even soften it with a smile. 'If you really wanted to break into business, Amelia, you'd already have done it—the movement on the motor deal would have been announced and neither of us would be sitting here now. You chose not to break that story, Amelia.'

'I know.' Huddling further into her dressing gown, Amelia gave a tired nod. 'I know I did.'

'So now you have to ask yourself why.'

Shooting him a baleful look, she let out a long drawn-out sigh, almost annoyed with him for making her admit her truth. 'I don't want the doors of big-business reporting to open,' Amelia responded hesitantly. 'In fact now the bolts are off I'm actually realising just how happy I am doing what I do.'

'Why?' Navy eyes pushed her to delve deeper. 'What is it about your work that you love?'

'The depth,' Amelia responded. 'My father would shudder if he heard me say that, but even though they might appear throwaway pieces they sustain interest, whereas in the business world my stories will be old by lunchtime. I'm always going to be chasing the next story, always stabbing people in the back and reporting on other people's misery.'

'Sounds to me like you've already made up your mind,' Vaughan suggested.

'Which should make things simple. But given that I'm covering a maternity leave position, and that the job I love doing is going to be over anyway, now really isn't the time to be upsetting the boss.' She gave a pale smile. 'The baby's already got teeth.'

Taking a sip of her chocolate, Amelia peered down at the dispersing patrons below, at tired waiters replacing crisp white cotton tablecloths, setting up for the new day that would surely dawn. The piano was quiet now, allowing her to mull over her own thoughts. She was grateful that Vaughan didn't jump in with another flash of insight, that he didn't attempt an answer when there really wasn't one.

'You're wrong about one thing, though.' Dragging her eyes back, Amelia broke the companionable silence. She had something she wanted to say. 'Journalists do have integrity, Vaughan—at least this one does.'

She waited—waited for him to apologise, to retract his rather sweeping generalisation—but instead he inhaled the brandy fumes from his glass before taking a long, slow sip.

'I guess we'll just have to wait and see.'

Placing her mug back on the table, Amelia felt her dressing gown part a fraction. Her hand moved to close it, but even in that tiny second she felt the shift, could almost feel the scorch marks where his eyes had burned her exposed flesh, was aware all over again of her attire, trying to fathom how without a word, with just one tiny motion, the atmosphere could dip so easily into dangerous territory.

'I'd better go.' Flustered now, she stood up, and so too did he, holding the French door open and following her from the balcony back inside his room.

Even though she'd only been there a short while ago it was unfamiliar all over again—the massive bed, somehow bigger, the air thick not with his cologne now, but with the thrum of heightened awareness. Her fingers refused to obey as she struggled with the unfamiliar lock on the door, and his hand made contact with hers as he moved to help. It was almost more than she could bear and still be expected to breathe. Amelia had to get out—had to get away from this overwhelming presence that spun her into confusion. But even with the door unlocked, even with her escape route open, still she couldn't move, trapped in her own desire.

Finally she looked up at him, and the desire in his eyes was like a mirror image of her own. Even if she didn't fit the usual dress code of the sophisticated women he attracted and discarded so easily she knew he was aroused, and it both thrilled and terrified her. But what was more overwhelming, more terrifying, was how much she wanted him—how much she longed for him to take her in his arms, to hush her troubled mind with a kiss. How very easy it would be to take that step over the mental line she had drawn, to again let her heart rule her head and let passion override sensibility.

Again.

Like a mental slap to her cheek, Taylor's brutal betrayal forced her mind to reality, allowed her legs to regain their function, her hands to pull open the door. She knew she had to get out—that she needed distance, clarity and recall.

Needed to recall the pain she had suffered before to remind her not to go there ever again.

'Goodnight, Vaughan.'

She attempted formal, attempted distance, but he swept it away without effort, one hand coming up to her arm. And despite the thick robe she could feel the heat of his palm on her skin, the space between them alive with thick tension. Every pore of her body flamed into response as he moved a fraction forward, moved into her personal space uninvited but unhindered, so close she could feel his breath on her cheeks. The weight of a kiss that simply had to happen was only a whisper away, and if her mind screamed no, then her body screamed yes.

His face moved in, but his lips teasingly missed hers, moving instead slowly along her cheek, the scratchy feel of him dragging against her, the weight of his swollen lips so close—summoning her to reciprocate if she dared, to seal this union. And she couldn't not.

Her lips turned to his like petals to the sun, and the blissful weight of his mouth was on hers. The cool control of his tongue was parting her lips, meeting the tip of hers, and slowly, coiling, chasing, relishing, she tasted the faint flavour of him, tasted the tang of brandy, tasted the decadent wine of his expert kiss. Every move of his lips, his tongue, was slow and deliberate, stirring the need within her with each skilful stroke. Her whole body was pitted with lust, arching towards him in necessary reaction—because she needed to feel him. One hand was guiding her as she moved, firmly nestled in the small of her back, and she felt as if he were touching her deep inside.

The hand that had captured her hair blazed a heated slow trail along her neck, a finger stilling for a second on the beat of her pulse as still he kissed her, still he drew her in. It was working down, ever down, so slowly she could have halted him at any moment, so slowly there was plenty of time to pull away to end this liaison—but it would have been easier to die than to end it now. She needed this, *needed* it in a primitive, deep, inexplicable way.

Her whole body was his willing instrument, preempting what was coming with dizzy need, so that when his hand slipped inside her robe her nipples were so taut, so achingly ready, a groan of sheer lustful pleasure welled in her mouth. It was drowned by his kiss as he rolled the engorged buds between his fingers, then took the weight of her bosom in his palm. His other hand was on her back, more urgent now, pushing her further towards him, till she could feel him, feel the solid beat of his arousal against her stomach.

Captured between the heat of his hand and the promise of his manhood, she felt the chirrup of the pulse between her legs more insistent now. Great

waves of lust were washing over her, and he could
have taken her there—she wanted him to take her
there. One kiss, one glimpse of his passion, one taste
of his promise and she wanted more—so why, Amelia
begged as she pulled her head back, was she ending
this? Why, when her body screamed for its just re-
wards, was her head telling her to stop?

'We can't.' Utterly unable to meet his eyes, she
attempted an explanation.

'We very nearly did,' Vaughan pointed out, his
hand still on the small of her back, his arousal still
solid against her, her own body still live with desire
in his arms. Wisps of passion still surged hopefully
through her veins and she pulled away more force-
fully now, snapping her robe together. But not quickly
enough to miss the weight of his gaze on the creamy
flesh of her breast. Her budding nipples were still jutting hopefully, and she knew he was taking it all in—
the glittering eyes, the flush of arousal on her
cheeks—knew how contrary her words sounded when
her body clearly wanted him.

'You don't mix business with pleasure, remember?'

She needed help here—needed Vaughan to take
some of the weight from her buckling shoulders, to
offer a voice of reason that would stave off the onslaught of disaster. But Vaughan wasn't helping.
Vaughan was only making it worse.

'I made the rule, Amelia. It's not yours to keep.'
A finger traced her cheekbone, drew around the con-
tours of her mouth, the pad of his thumb nudging the
flesh still swollen from his kiss. She ached to relent,
to part her lips on his command, to resume this de-

licious liaison—but she had to be strong, couldn't do this again and hope to come out intact.

'It's a good rule.' Snapping into business mode, she attempted a brittle smile. 'And one I intend to keep.'

'So what was that, then?'

'A goodnight kiss,' Amelia attempted. 'Vaughan, it was just a kiss.'

'Just a kiss?' The preposterousness of her statement was there in his voice. 'Tell me, Amelia, do you kiss all your subjects like that?'

'Of course not.' Amelia was flustered, unsure how to respond here, and lying was easier. Keeping her distance was safer than letting him glimpse her uncertainty, letting him see her naked truth.

How could she tell a man who could only break her heart that in a single kiss he had moved her beyond distraction? That it was taking every shred of strength she could summon to keep her hand on the door? That she had to physically force herself not to run to him?

'It's just safer, that's all…' Her mouth snapped closed as she instantly regretted her choice of words, wishing she could somehow retract them. But they were already out there, already being processed in that astute mind, already being hurled back at her. She braced herself for defence.

'Safer?'

'Yes—safer,' Amelia snapped back, more angry with herself than him, because with one single word she had allowed him to see her fears. 'Safer than doing something stupid in the heat of a moment when we'd both surely regret it in the morning.'

'Why do you assume we'd regret it?'

'Because…' a tiny nervous laugh, a silent plea with her eyes '…it's just not me, Vaughan. I can't be your lover for a night or a week—can't just give you a piece of myself, knowing it isn't going to last.'

'And you know that for sure, do you?'

He was moving in on her again, hands leaning against the wall on either side of her head—the master with the key, creating a prison she wasn't sure she wanted to escape from.

'I know that you want me, Vaughan, and I know that I want you. But…'

'Why does there have to be one?' His voice was so low, so raw she had to strain to catch it. 'How do you know that we won't still feel this way tomorrow?'

He was moving in to kiss her, moving in for the final delicious kill, and Amelia only knew she had to stop him—had to hit him with her final defence. 'Because you're Vaughan Mason.'

His hands dropped to his sides and she could have walked away. But she felt stronger now—strong enough to see this through

'Because I've got a past you mean?'

'No, Vaughan, because *I've* got a past. I know your type…'

'My type?'

'Yes, your type, Vaughan. The type of man who attracts women, who likes women, who effortlessly attracts them and for a while adores them until just as effortlessly he moves on.'

'Now who's doing the sweeping generalisations?' Vaughan sneered. 'So what? You want commitment before you sleep with someone? Is that what you're saying?'

'No, I just know—'

'Know what?' Vaughan broke in. 'That I'm a bastard? That I'm setting you up for a fall?'

'Not deliberately, perhaps…' She shook her head in an attempt to clear it. 'Vaughan, this won't last—you surely know that. And I'm not going to allow myself to get involved with a man who can only hurt me in the end.'

'You think you've got me all worked out. You've read my bio and from that you know me. Well, I'm not some doped-up popstar with an ego that needs feeding.'

So brutal were his words that she felt as if she'd been hit—appalled that he knew, and that somehow he'd worked out so much from so very little.

'How—?' The word strangled in her throat, 'How could you know that?'

'I can read you, Amelia.' His low husky voice reached her ears. 'But don't worry, I'm not going to *make* you do what you *want* to. I'm not going to beg for something we both know you want. But think about this when you creep into that cold bed alone—just think about this as you lie there staring at the ceiling: any man you feel for could ultimately hurt you; any man who can make your body respond the way it just did could one day use it against you. So if you're looking for iron-clad guarantees, if you're looking to safeguard your heart against pain, you can kiss goodbye to passion.'

And even though he didn't move, not by a hair, he

made love to her all over again. His eyes were almost black as he stared down at her body, the navy obscured by his dilated pupils, scorching through the robe she gripped tightly in her trembling hand. So bold was his stare she could almost feel his hand again on her breast, feel the champagne bubbles of arousal fizzing, and she ran a nervous tongue over her lips. Only it didn't help. The delicious taste of him was still there in her mouth. It was as if he held the remote control to her body—he pushed her buttons, turning her on at will and she only knew that she had to get out.

This time she meant it. Wrenching open the door and fleeing down the passage, she only breathed when her own door was safely closed behind her. Her body burned with dissatisfaction, her emotions utterly violated by his brutal words—and damn him, Amelia realised, he was right.

Creeping into bed, she lay there, supremely aware of him just as few metres away, on the other side of the flimsy hotel wall, her whole body burning with a desire she'd chosen to starve in the name of preservation, staring appalled at the life that lay before her.

A life without passion.

A life that was safe.

CHAPTER FIVE

'GOOD morning!' Her greeting rang out loudly as Vaughan made his way over to the breakfast table—one of the same tables they'd idly watched being laid up only hours ago.

The piano stood proud and silent now—no gentle background noise to fill this difficult moment as the restaurant area slowly filled up with bleary-eyed early risers and crisp businessmen and women grabbing a caffeine fix before they headed for the office. Melbourne was stirring into life after a long sultry night.

She said her greeting again when he sat down, and again Vaughan didn't respond—didn't even acknowledge the smile she'd firmly painted on this morning—instead sitting down and signalling to the waiter to fill his coffee cup.

She'd been determined to get in first and set the tone, put last night firmly behind them and resume normal services. But, Amelia realized as Vaughan sat down and scowled at his newspaper, not even bothering to thank the waiter who had promptly filled his cup, there had been no need to rush to greet him—Vaughan, it would appear, wasn't in a hurry to talk to anyone. Sulky and broody, he stared at his paper, his only movement an occasional hand reaching out for his coffee.

'Did you sleep well?' Amelia attempted, ready to rip the bloody paper from his hands if that was what it took, utterly determined to get this over with.

'No.' Navy eyes peered over the top of his paper. 'Are you going to try and tell me that you did?'

God, why did he have to be so direct? Why couldn't he act like any normal person and pretend that last night's events simply hadn't happened?

'I did, actually,' Amelia lied, spooning sugar into her tea and getting most of it on the table. She damn well wasn't going to tell him she'd spent the night pinned to the bed, simultaneously reeling at her boldness, her utter stupidity for going into his room so inappropriately dressed, for responding to his kisses with such blatant ease, yet all the while berating herself for terminating it.

His words had stung her to the core. All night she'd played them over in her mind—too terrified to flick on the kettle in case he heard her, reluctant to go out on the balcony in case he saw her. Knowing that with one crook of his manicured finger she'd run to him, that with one more taste of that decadent mouth she'd fall into his bed with nothing to save her.

'Vaughan—please!' Still she spoke to the sports page. 'If this is about last night…' She held her breath as the paper slowly dropped, his eyes frowning as he met hers. 'If this silent treatment—'

'Silent treatment?' He shook his head, a mirthless

smile almost evident on his taut lips, then to her utter fury lifted the paper again and proceeded to read.

'Look, if this is going to affect our working relationship…'

'Amelia, on reflection you made a very valid point last night.' Vaughan slowly folded up his paper and placed it on the table beside him as she sat squirming with embarrassment. He stretched out her discomfort for as long as possible before finally continuing. 'Perhaps people *should* get to know each other before they sleep together. Maybe people *should* know that just because someone chooses not to bounce across to the breakfast table squawking like a galah, it doesn't mean that they're ruing the fact they didn't get their rocks off last night, but that they are quite simply people who like at least a few micrograms of caffeine in their system before they enter into a deep and meaningful discussion.'

'Getting your rocks off?' Amelia sneered, embarrassed at her overreaction, yet sure, quite sure, that she had been right—that Vaughan 'in control' Mason was seriously rattled because, unlike most women, she hadn't succumbed to his undeniably skilful charms. 'I made more than one valid point last night, Vaughan. And a man who refers to it as "getting his rocks off" really isn't the type of guy I want to be sharing a bed with.'

'And a woman who refers to sex as "it" clearly doesn't know how to enjoy herself!'

'So I'm frigid, am I?'

She saw the tiny upward flicker of his eyebrow,

knew that she had shocked him slightly, but years spent in journalism had taught Amelia not to shy away from embarrassing subjects, to face tough conversations head-on. This was tough, supremely difficult, but she was damn well going to see it through.

'Are you trying to say that because I—heaven forbid—chose not to sleep with you it means that deep down I can't really like sex very much? That it has nothing to do with the fact that I didn't want to be yet another notch on your well-worn bedpost? Does the fact I demand more of myself than to be another of your conquests mean, according to your fragile male ego, that I don't really like *it* very much at all? Oh, sorry,' Amelia snarled a correction, 'you don't like that word, do you? I meant to say—'

'I get the picture.' A hand shot up to stop her. He was clearly embarrassed at her boldness, for once looking anything other than cool. 'Look, let's just forget it, shall we?'

'That's what I was trying to do this morning,' Amelia pointed out. 'For your information, I'm not a morning person either.'

'Can we please start again?' Vaughan asked, and after a moment on her high horse Amelia relented.

'Good morning, Vaughan.'

'Good morning, Amelia. Did you sleep well?'

'Actually, no. How about you?'

'Terribly.' He slipped in one tiny cheat. 'I had, er, rather pressing things on my mind.' Seeing her cheeks darken he finally gave in with an apologetic smile.

'Would you think that I was avoiding you if I said I need to ditch you for the morning.'

'Of course not.' Amelia shrugged. 'Like I said, I was surprised how many meetings I got into yesterday. Anyway, I've got plenty of work I should be doing.'

'What if I also said that I need to speak with Mr Cheng alone this afternoon?'

Peeling open a croissant with slightly shaky hands and spooning jam onto it, she gave a pale smile. 'Then I'd be starting to think that maybe you are avoiding me after all. Not really.' She smiled when she saw his slightly worried frown. 'Vaughan, I always knew there would be things I couldn't come along to. I'm not a child you have to amuse for the day. I'll be completely fine.'

'We could meet for lunch—' He gave a small wince almost before the sentence was out.

'Except…?' Amelia said for him.

'I've just remembered that I've arranged to meet someone.' He hesitated for longer than usual, his frown deepening, then eyed her cautiously, as if weighing up whether or not to continue. 'I suppose you could come, but given your career revelations, how off the record is off the record?'

'It's completely non-negotiable,' Amelia replied, utterly without hesitation. 'Your secrets are safe with me. They just help.' Realising he didn't understand, she elaborated slightly. 'Help me to form a picture in my mind. But just because I know something it doesn't mean I have to reveal it.'

'You're quite sure about that?'

He'd really piqued her interest now. For the first time he was cagey and hesitant, and it only served to intrigue her more, but Amelia knew when to hold back, knew when to feign uninterest—at least when it was about work. 'Look, you do your lunch and I'll catch up with you later this evening—tomorrow, even. It really isn't a big deal.'

'I'm meeting with one of the directors of a children's hospital.' Vaughan grimaced slightly, as if he regretted even saying it. 'Every year I give a small donation.'

'So small that they take you out for lunch when you're in town?' Amelia said shrewdly.

'Okay, a *significant* donation,' Vaughan admitted reluctantly. 'The thing is, Sam, he's the director, is doing his best to persuade me to go public with my support.'

'Why don't you?' Amelia asked, her tone completely matter of fact. 'Almost every celebrity I've ever interviewed has done the rounds of the children's wards to soften their image.'

'Exactly,' Vaughan replied, his voice suddenly curt. 'But I'm hardly a celebrity.'

'But you are, Vaughan,' Amelia pointed out. 'You're good-looking, impossibly rich, reeking of scandal and still single! Take it from a woman who knows—you're a celebrity! Why don't you want me to use this? Heaven knows, a piece of good publicity couldn't hurt you right now.'

'So I should ask a couple of sick kids to pose with me?'

'You wouldn't be the first,' Amelia responded. 'And you would be doing some good—it might make a few other business magnates dig deeper.'

'So why not get the mileage?'

Now it was Amelia feeling shallow, all of a sudden uncomfortable with the conversation.

'Those children don't know me, Amelia. I'm not some popstar they adore, waltzing onto the ward for a photo shoot. I'm just a guy in a suit…'

'Who donates a lot of money.' She saw his lips tighten. 'Come on, Vaughan. A significant amount to you would be a fortune to most people. And maybe the children won't know you, but their parents will…'

'I'm sure if their child's sick enough to be there they'll have other things on their mind. Amelia this is something I do because I want to—something just for me. That's what I'm going to explain to Sam to-day. He's hoping that if I go public it might trigger a few more in the business community to get involved.'

'Which can surely only be a good thing?' Amelia answered, still not entirely convinced.

She'd heard too many celebrities insisting this was something they wanted to do, been to too many contrived charity dos for a cynical edge not to have evolved. And if that sounded hard, she didn't care. At the end of the day the hospitals needed the money and Vaughan needed the positive publicity—it was win-win as far as Amelia was concerned.

'If you're so intent on it being kept private, then why are you asking me along? Why are you asking a *journalist* to an intensely private lunch.'

'You don't mince your words, do you?' Vaughan smiled almost reluctantly.

'I don't like being fed a line.' Amelia shrugged, happier now they were on safer ground. She was back—maybe not back at the driver's wheel, but at least up in the passenger seat, shoulder to shoulder with this complicated man.

For as long as it took for her second up of coffee to be poured!

'I listened to what you said about the bigger picture. I figure that an hour in Sam's company might bring you on board, and an up-and-coming journalist on side can only be a good thing for the hospital.'

'Oh.'

Placing a hand over his cup, he refused a refill, waiting till the waiter had walked away before standing up.

'Can I let the restaurant know to expect one more?'

An *extremely* significant donation might have been a better description, Amelia decided as she handed over her jacket and stepped into the restaurant. Wafts of herbs and garlic filled the air, along with the pop of corks, and there was the luxurious feel of deep carpet beneath her feet. Small donations surely didn't merit this five-star treatment.

A frown formed as Amelia glanced over to Vaughan's table and then at her watch. Vaughan had specifically told her one p.m. and she was five minutes early—yet already he and his companion were clearly at the coffee stage.

'Amelia.' The consummate host, Vaughan stood up and greeted her, introducing her to Sam and guiding her to a seat. 'I'm sorry about this, but something came up and we had to switch times.'

'My fault, I'm afraid,' Sam apologised, while not looking remotely sorry. 'I've got an afternoon appointment which means that I'm going to have to wrap this up.'

'Now that you've got what you wanted,' Vaughan said dryly, and Amelia frowned at the rather obvious irritation in his voice.

'You'll be great, Vaughan.' Sam grinned. 'It's for the kids, remember?' He smiled over to Amelia. 'It was a pleasure to meet you, Miss Jacobs. Hopefully we'll see you at the charity auction on Thursday.'

Glancing briefly over, she saw Vaughan shake his head, his eyes demanding her to say no. But in a curiously defiant gesture she smiled at the rather pushy Sam.

'Is that an invitation?'

'It certainly is.' Sam beamed. 'We can use all the publicity we can get. Don't worry, Vaughan—' his wide smile wasn't reciprocated '—you'll be just fine. Oh, and before I forget—do you have those tickets you promised?'

Unclipping his briefcase, Vaughan pulled out a stiff white envelope, handing it over to Sam before shaking his hand and bidding him goodbye.

'Well, that was enlightening,' Amelia said with more than a vague hint of sarcasm as Marcus walked off. 'I'll certainly get a lot of mileage out of that lunch.'

'Bloody salesmen,' Vaughan snapped at the departing back.

'I thought he was one of the directors from the hospital.'

'He's in the wrong job, then,' Vaughan clipped, but he didn't elaborate further.

Amelia's curiosity was seriously piqued. She felt as if she'd rushed in at the end of something and missed the important part—like watching her favourite soap without knowing what had happened last week.

'What was in the envelope?' Amelia asked, but Vaughan didn't even attempt an explanation.

'Have something to eat.'

'I'm actually not that hungry, Vaughan. If you didn't want me here, you should have just said.'

'Sam rescheduled at the last moment,' Vaughan argued.

Amelia fished in her bag, frowning as she pulled out her mobile. 'I can't see your message here, Vaughan.'

'Because there isn't one,' Vaughan responded easily, completely ignoring her sarcasm. 'There isn't one because I knew if I tried to reschedule then you'd assume I was making excuses and wouldn't come.'

'You were right,' Amelia clipped. 'But only about the fact I wouldn't have come. Vaughan, I do have an article to write. I've dragged myself through the city for a meal I don't really want to sit with a person I'll no doubt be seeing this evening.'

'I thought the entire purpose of this exercise was to get to know me better,' Vaughan retorted, flashing a triumphant smile.

'*Attempting* to get to know you better,' Amelia corrected. 'You don't exactly give much away. It's like pulling teeth without an anaesthetic, trying to extract information from you. Everything I manage to glean you counter with an ''off the record'' reminder.'

'Oh, come on, Amelia.' Vaughan gave her a look that showed her he was anything but moved. 'If you can't fashion a story after all the meetings you've been in, then you're not the journalist I thought you were. You don't have to name names all the time.'

'It's not them I'm interested in, though,' Amelia retorted. 'I meant what I said last night. It's a portrayal of you that I want to do, not a bloody business piece.' She took a deep breath, shook her head as the waiter handed her a menu.

The truth of the matter was she was struggling with contrary emotions. As much as she wanted to get to know him better, as much as she needed more information to write the piece she really wanted to write, she was terrified of being alone with him again—had been secretly relieved at the chance to spend a day licking her wounds and hopefully fashioning her brain into some sort of order before the next onslaught of emotional torture Vaughan so easily generated. She'd needed the space to get her head together, to ring a girlfriend and beg for sensibility before she surely caved in. A business lunch she could just about have dealt with, but an hour or two up close and personal with Vaughan Mason was way too much for her shredded emotions right now.

'Come on—have something,' Vaughan pushed, retrieving the menu and placing it in front of her. 'You can't come all this way and not eat.'

But the thought of chasing spaghetti around her plate in her present state, with Vaughan calmly watching on, wasn't particularly palatable.

'I'd far rather have a sandwich sent up to my hotel room,' Amelia resisted, hoisting her bag up onto her shoulder. 'I know you're busy, Vaughan, and, as I said this morning, you really don't have to babysit me—this was a business lunch that should have been rescheduled, not a date you've somehow managed to break and need to make up for. A phone call would have sufficed.'

'We could share a cheese platter,' Vaughan responded, completely dismissing her entire statement, obviously happy with *his* choice and clicking his fingers to summon the waiter, not even bothering to check if it was okay with Amelia.

'I could have a raving lactose intolerance,' Amelia bristled. 'I could blow up like a soccerball at the mere sight of cheese!'

'Do you?'

'No, but that isn't the point.'

Despite his bland expression, she knew he was laughing at her.

'Would you care for some wine?' Vaughan checked. 'Or does that bring you out in hives?'

'Water will be fine.'

'So, what have you written about me so far?'

Amelia nearly knocked over her glass at his way too direct question.

'Am I allowed to look?'

'No!' Perish the thought.

Amelia gave a visible shudder. The thought of anyone reading her work at this stage filled her with horror, but it had nothing to do with what she'd written—was more the complete lack of it. Though she damn well wasn't going to tell anyone that she'd barely got past the first paragraph, that her mind was constantly wandering. This whole morning, when she should have been working, had been spent reluctantly recalling the sheer heady bliss of being held by him, and, as intimate as she wanted her piece to be, she certainly wasn't about to share *that* with her readers.

'That bad, huh?'

'Worse,' Amelia said with a teasing smile. 'Actually, I haven't touched on your appalling arrogance yet. I'm saving that for this afternoon's session.'

'Maybe you should have some wine after all. It might help soften the edges a bit.'

'Come on, Vaughan,' Amelia moaned. 'You have to give me something here. What's this about a charity auction on Thursday?'

'I'm the auctioneer,' Vaughan sighed, and Amelia finally started to laugh.

'This I have to see!'

Vaughan rolled his eyes. 'Please let's not talk about it. And even if I have to strap you to the bed, there's no way you're coming to watch.'

Ouch!

As innocent as it had been, in their present rather fragile state any mention of bed had them both inwardly cringing. And, though she couldn't be sure, Amelia could have sworn she saw the first hint of a blush darken his cheeks at the small *faux pas*.

'But I've been invited.' Amelia grinned, enjoying his moment of discomfort. 'I wouldn't dream of missing it! So what's it in aid of? The children's hospital?'

'Actually, it's the cystic fibrosis unit holding it. Apparently they urgently need to purchase some piece of equipment, but the budget has already been allocated for this financial year, so rather than waiting they've decided to bite the bullet and raise the money themselves.'

'And what's your role in this? Apart from being the auctioneer?' Amelia grinned again. 'I assume that was a last-minute addition?'

'You assume correctly. I donated a holiday—that envelope contained the tickets—ten nights for two in Fiji at a luxury resort…' He smiled as Amelia let out a blissful sigh.

'With air tickets?' she checked, pouting with not so feigned jealousy as Vaughan nodded.

'You'd think that would have sufficed. But, not happy with that, Sam decided to bully me into standing with a microphone, making a complete idiot of myself.'

'I can't believe you'd ever be bullied into something you didn't want to do.'

Spreading creamy thick cheese onto a pepper cracker, she looked up to see him smiling again.

'What?'

'For a lactose intolerant person who's not particularly hungry you're doing a good job with that cheese. Don't stop,' he added when she put down her cracker. 'I'm just glad I'm forgiven, that's all.'

'You're not.' Amelia grinned.

'And you'll never be forgiven, young lady, if you even so much as smile at my efforts on Thursday night.'

'I can't believe you're so worked up about it.' Amelia laughed. 'Surely you're used to public speaking? I can't believe you'd get worked up about some tiny cocktail party for a children's ward.'

'I'm not getting worked up,' Vaughan snapped, then relented with a brief nod. 'I just can't really picture myself working an audience, telling them to dig deep for the kids. I'm not the world's most effusive person.'

Oh, but he was!

Staring across the table, glimpsing again that bland inscrutable face, it was hard to believe the passion that had smoldered last night—how the eyes that were guarded now had burned with fervour, how his demonstrative hands had expressed without words so many simmering feelings, how she had witnessed first hand the hidden depths of this extraordinary man.

'How did he do it?'

She was deep in thought and his question caught her off guard. Two vertical lines appeared on the bridge of her nose as she realised the conversation had shifted to strictly personal, and that once again the subject was her.

'How did Taylor Dean get that suspicious, cynical woman to relent?'

'I don't want to talk about it.'

'I do.' Vaughan leant over the table, the motion causing his knees to brush hers, and he held his legs there, trapped her at the table with a mere touch. 'I can't imagine you of all people falling for a popstar. You're not exactly…'

'Stunning?' Amelia offered, but immediately he shook his head.

'You have the self-esteem of an ant, Amelia. I was about to say you're not exactly groupie material. I just can't picture you falling for a line.'

'It wasn't a line.' Amelia blinked back at him and he saw the pain in her eyes, saw the swirling confusion still there. The pain was obviously still new. 'At the risk of sounding like an even bigger fool, I actually think he did love me.' She took a gulp of her water. 'Hard to imagine, I guess.'

'No.' His voice was husky and thoughtful, the flip, slightly patronizing tone gone now, and he stared back at her—stared back and willed her to open up. 'No, it isn't actually that hard to imagine someone falling completely head over heels in love with you, Amelia. Can you tell me what happened between you and Taylor?'

He watched her face stiffen, the creamy shoulders tighten. But if it hurt to probe he didn't care. Insatiable curiosity was burning within, that this wary, suspicious woman could ever have succumbed to the negligible charms of a man like Taylor.

'Why?' Amelia begged. But she already knew the answer—knew that he needed to understand why she held back. And maybe by telling him, so might she.

'I was booked to do an interview. I had an hour slot with him. But there was a PA by his side—not a chance of digging deeper. Every time I asked something that wasn't on the list, every time I veered off course, his PA broke in—which was annoying, but expected. It happens all the time during interviews. Only suddenly it wasn't me getting annoyed. All of a sudden it was Taylor who was frowning at the interruptions. It was as if he really wanted to talk to me—really wanted to finally be honest. In the end he asked his PA to leave.'

Vaughan could see the tension burning in her eyes, the bat of her lids as she blinked in disbelief at her own recall.

'I thought at the time it was because he wanted to talk, wanted to open up some more and give some honest answers for the article. I never for a moment imagined he actually wanted to get to know me.'

'How long did you see him for?'

'A few months.' Amelia gave a tight shrug. 'Which, in the scheme of things, isn't long at all. But when I fall, I fall...'

'And you fell?' Vaughan checked gently.

'Hook, line and sinker. But…' She took a deep breath, the shame and humiliation that she'd been so naïve burning as she retold her story. 'But so did he. He was always asking me to come and watch him perform. But with work and everything more often than not I was too busy. One day I decided to surprise him. He was singing in Brisbane and I decided what the hell? So I jumped on a plane and headed over. His PA tried to stop me from going into his hotel room…but I went in anyway. I don't think I have to spell out what I saw…'

'I'm sorry.'

'So was Taylor.' Maybe she should have had some wine after all. Recalling this was too painful for a Tuesday afternoon. 'Devastated, actually. And I think it was genuine. He's just too used to having too much of a good thing and too weak to say no. He swore he'd never cheat on me again, and maybe he believed it—maybe he believed at the time he was speaking the truth. But by then it didn't matter.'

'No second chance?'

Amelia shook her head. 'Not for that. I think I must have been the first woman to ever dump him. He still rings, still sends flowers, still tries to convince me he's changed.'

'What if he has?'

'Too late.' Amelia shook her head firmly, but she saw the flicker of doubt in his eyes and it annoyed her. 'It's over, Vaughan. How could I ever trust him again? How could I ever forgive him? It has to be over.'

'But you still have feelings?'

Oh, she had feelings. Feelings so raw they hurt. But not for Taylor. She'd ripped him out of her mind as easily as a teenager tearing down a poster. Infidelity was the one sin she could never forgive. The hurt, pain and emotion were still there, yet she was learning to live with them. But, no, it wasn't her feelings for Taylor that terrified her now. It was her feelings for Vaughan—the one man who could do it to her all over again if she let him. The one man who could snake into her heart, into her bed. And quite simply she couldn't bear to let him in just to watch him leave, couldn't begin to imagine moving on from the devastation he would surely wreak, couldn't bear to build her world from ground zero all over again.

'I'm not a popstar, Amelia.'

His voice was as gentle as she'd ever heard it. She could still feel the weight of his knees against hers, feel his dry, hot hand coiling around her fingers, tempting her back to the forbidden garden where only last night she'd strayed.

'I'm just a guy in a suit…'

'You know that you're not.' Tears glittered in her eyes. She felt as if she'd been swimming against the tide for ever, swimming towards a bobbing life raft in the ocean only to find out it was a shark. 'We're from different worlds, Vaughan. You just want what you can't have, and I'm sorry if it sounds boring, but from a relationship I want more.'

'Such as?'

'Safety.' Taking a deep breath, she laid it on the

line. The fact that she'd only known him a few days was irrelevant when she was staring down the barrel of a gun aimed at her heart. 'And if that sounds boring too then I make no apology. I've tried the fast lane and I didn't like it. Next time I give my heart away, Vaughan, I want the lot—marriage, kids, a partner to stand shoulder to shoulder with. A man I can trust, not someone always on the lookout for the next good thing, not someone whose ego needs constantly massaging.'

'And is anything on that list negotiable?'

She could see a muscle flickering in his cheek, feel the tension in his body, his knees pressing into hers more urgently as he awaited her answer.

'I want the lot, Vaughan,' Amelia repeated, shaking her head.

It was as if a pin had been pushed into a balloon. The tension in the air dispersed, and the pressure on her knees was removed as Vaughan flashed her a very false smile.

'And you deserve it.' For the longest time his eyes sought hers, before finally they dragged away. His guard was back up, the shutters firmly down, and whatever she had said to make him keep his distance had worked a charm, because it was a stranger on the other side of the table now. Every shred of intimacy was suddenly gone. 'You deserve every bit of it, Amelia. Don't settle for anything less.'

'I won't…' Tears were pricking now, horrible hot tears she would never let him see.

Making her excuses, Amelia fled for the safety of

the washroom, where she stared at her reflection in the mirror for an age, mentally scolding herself for daring to hope.

As if Vaughan wanted the same thing—as if allowing him to glimpse her dreams would mean for a moment that he wanted to share them.

Go for it, he'd basically told her. *Only not with me.*

Thank God for face powder, Amelia thought ruefully. And thank God for lipgloss to add sparkle to a rather strained smile. And as she made her way back to the table suddenly her mind was back on the job, her eyes narrowing in recognition as she watched a gentleman leaving the restaurant, eyes cast downwards, collar firmly up, clearly not wanting to be seen.

'Everything okay?'

Perhaps sensing her distraction, Vaughan eyed her with concern as she sat back down at the table, watching as she pushed a nod while nibbling nervously on her bottom lip. Those delicious eyes were distant as her hands reached out for a glass of water.

'You look as if you've just seen a ghost.'

CHAPTER SIX

'WHAT the hell was Carter doing at the restaurant?'

The one time she actually needed to speak to Paul he was completely unavailable. It had taken the best part of forty-eight hours to finally get him on the line.

'I have no idea.' Paul sighed. 'Perhaps he was hungry?'

'Don't play games with me, Paul.'

Two days of being put on hold and speaking into his message bank had taken its toll, coupled with the fact that, judging from the frenzied activities going on in the bar on the ground floor, her and Vaughan's idea of a cocktail party clearly differed.

The tiny informal gathering Amelia had foolishly predicted was clearly way off the mark. Every time she had graced the foyer today she had been greeted with the sight of a closed-off area and endless staff carrying fresh flowers and boxes into its dark depths. Even Vaughan had swanned down to the hotel's health spa in his white toweling robe—no doubt to have a shave and a facial and manicure, Amelia thought. If only she'd been able to pack Shelly!

Paul giving her the runaround wasn't helping her already frazzled nerves, and now, throwing both caution and possibly her career to the wind, Amelia let rip along the phone line to Sydney.

'Paul, we both know Carter's barely human. Why

would he need food when he survives solely on other people's misery? Why didn't he come over and introduce himself? I need to know what's going on. I need to know what it is you've got on Vaughan.'

'No, Amelia, you don't.' Paul's voice was non-negotiable. 'I know and that's enough. You just do your job and let me do mine. Keep right on buttering him up and get what you can out of him.'

'This isn't Chinese Torture I'm playing at here, Paul. I'm writing an article on the man, for heaven's sake, not preparing a case for the prosecution.'

'Carter said that you two were very cosy in the restaurant.' Completely unmoved by her vehement denial, Paul pushed harder. 'What were you talking about?'

'Nothing that would interest you, Paul.'

'Try me,' Paul insisted.

'As I said, it's nothing that would interest you, because we were actually talking about *me*.'

Replacing the receiver, Amelia saw that her hand was shaking. The horrible truth was starting to creep in. Her supposed big break hadn't just fallen into her lap. It had been calculated every step of the way. Carter hadn't hot-footed it to Canberra to follow the election trail. Thumbing through her pile of newspapers, Amelia confirmed what she already knew. Carter hadn't filed a single report. He had disappeared so that Amelia would interview Vaughan.

Dragging in air, Amelia tried to make sense of it all, tried to conjure an explanation. But nothing was forthcoming. Picking up the telephone immediately when it buzzed again, hoping against hope that it was

Paul with some answers, she jumped out of her guilty skin when she realised it was Vaughan, in an unusually relaxed mode.

'The staff were wondering what time you're coming down. You didn't book a time.'

'Coming down?' Amelia frowned into the phone.

'To the health spa. If you want to have a massage and your make-up done, you really ought to step on it!'

'Oh!' Amelia chewed nervously on her bottom lip, almost whimpering at the delicious thought of a massage and facial before she braved the cool stares of Melbourne's most elite. But, given her rather shaky relationship with her credit card at the moment she could hardly justify it—and Paul certainly wasn't going to sign it off as a necessary claim. 'I was just going to have a bath up here.'

'Well, do you want them to come up to your room?' Vaughan asked, with all the arrogance of the truly rich.

'I can run my own bath, Vaughan,' Amelia answered testily. 'And I've had years of practice with a mascara wand.'

'Fine,' Vaughan clipped. 'It just seems a shame to waste it when it's included in the room. I'll let them know you won't be—'

'It's included in the room?' Amelia swallowed her squeal of delight, trying to sound as nonchalant as possible as she punched the air in joy. 'Oh, well, in that case it *would* be a shame to waste it. Tell them I'll be right down.'

Vaughan was just leaving as Amelia arrived, grinning from ear to ear in her towelling robe. Like a child let loose in a sweet shop, she ran her eye along the impressive list of treatments.

'Do you have any plans this afternoon?' Amelia checked. 'Anything I ought to…?'

'Nothing.' Vaughan smiled. 'Take your time. You deserve an afternoon off.'

Oh, she did, Amelia thought wickedly. She decided there and then to have everything on the list—well, maybe not everything, Amelia mentally corrected, as the stragglers on her eyebrows were waxed away in seconds.

Brazilians must have a markedly high pain threshold!

Whoever had said that money didn't buy happiness certainly hadn't spent two hours in this hotel's health spa being wrapped in mud, massaged, pummelled and exfoliated to within an inch of their lives, hadn't felt the sheer bliss of a scalp massage, nor lain in a reclining chair as their finger and toenails were simultaneously painted, hadn't known the sheer heady pleasure of staring down at two newly pretty feet that were finally actually fit for the jewelled impulse-bought sandals awaiting their mistress at the bottom of her suitcase in the top floor of the hotel! Absolute bliss!

Stepping out of the lift, padding along the floor towards her room, Amelia felt good enough about herself to smile at the stunning woman walking towards her, clouds of dark hair billowing over her shoulders, wafting a perfume that Amelia could never afford. She was more than happy to impart just a touch of her buoyant mood, and shrugged to herself when the smile wasn't reciprocated, when the rather haunted-looking beauty pointedly avoided her gaze and walked swiftly past.

Only as she reached her room did the smile fade from Amelia's face. The heady perfume that had filled the corridor was noticeably absent now, but Amelia knew, just knew, where the haunted beauty had come from.

Heart in her mouth, she retraced her steps, closing her newly made-up eyes in regret as she reached Vaughan's closed door, inhaling the heady fragrance.

Money did buy happiness.

The blissfully decadent two hours she'd just spent meant nothing now. The health spa *hadn't* been included in her room…

Vaughan had conveniently got rid of her.

She sat on her bed, huddled into her robe, staring unseeing into space, appalled at the jealousy that assailed her. A full hour had passed—a full hour watching the shadows on the wall lengthen, a full hour berating herself for even daring to dream that someone like Vaughan could ever really change and, more pathetically, that she, Amelia, might be the one to change him.

She should be getting ready!

Amelia winced as she glanced at her watch, and her expression blew into a full-face grimace as a pounding on the door forced her attention. She pulled off her robe and poured herself into her dress in record time, and headed to open the door.

'Can you sew?'

It wasn't the greeting Amelia was expecting when she opened the door to impatient knocking.

Her lilac strappy dress really deserved the garnish of a strapless bra and heels before it was seen—not, Amelia realised, that Vaughan would notice in his current state. She flattened herself against the wall as he strode impatiently in.

Wired to the max, he practically marched into her room, impossibly restless but still beautiful in a charcoal suit, his shirt impossibly white, a dark grey silk tie hanging around an unbuttoned shirt.

'Well, sewing's not something I pride myself on,' Amelia responded, deliberately missing the point. If he wanted her to sew for him then he could damn well ask her properly!

'I've lost my top button.' Vaughan attempted an explanation. 'Housekeeping said they'd send someone to mend it, but that's going to take for ever. I'm supposed to be down there in five minutes.'

'Here.' Smiling sweetly, she picked up the miniature sewing kit that hotels always provided, handing it to him and watching his frown deepen. 'You can use this.'

He didn't say it, but Amelia swore she could hear the irritated curse that was on the tip of his tongue. 'Amelia—' Taking a deep breath, attempting a pleasant smile, Vaughan tried again. 'Would you mind sewing my top button on for me?' He held up his arms to reveal two shiny silver cufflinks. 'I haven't got time to take my shirt off. Please,' he added, completely as an afterthought, as still she stood there.

'Seeing as you asked so nicely—' Amelia smiled '—then I'm sure I can manage a button.'

Or she should have been able to. It wasn't as if she had to rummage for a needle—one was provided, threaded, even, in the little kit the hotel provided— but he was too tall, too close, and way, way too near. She fumbled with the neck of his shirt, tried to keep her breathing even, tried to ignore the full mouth just a breath away.

'What did you do while I was gone?' Amelia asked lightly, way too lightly, holding her breath, mentally begging for an explanation—and dying a bit inside as she heard him lie.

'Slept.' Vaughan shrugged.

His skin was deliciously smooth, yet the blue-black suggestion of tomorrow lay just beneath the surface. Horribly clumsy, Amelia managed to push the needle through the stiff fabric without major incident, missing his jugular by mere centimeters. Her hand was shaking so much, and she knew that for the rest of her life, because of this moment, never again would she perform this minor task without remembering the scent, the feel, the sheer lusty presence of this man.

How easy it would be to just give in, to allow herself the luxury of even only once letting him in.

'Done.'

Slamming that door closed, Amelia stepped back.

He nodded his thanks, and a completely steady hand knotted his tie. Amelia vanished into the bathroom, her own hand not quite so steady as she touched up her lipstick and squeezed her feet into impossibly high shoes, before eyeing her reflection in the mirror. She was almost pleased with her appearance, almost pleased with the reflection that stared back at her. Except for the sight of two jiggling bosoms that really needed support.

If she'd had the courage to wander into the living room and rescue the offending article from her case she would have. But with Vaughan firmly *in situ* Amelia decided to risk going without. Rearranging her rather ample décolletage, and squirting another quick layer of perfume, she braced herself to face him in the bedroom.

'Shall we go down?'

She started speaking before she even left the bathroom, deliberately not looking at him as she set about packing her small evening bag, throwing in a lipstick and her room card. But she burned with awareness. It was the first time they'd been in a bedroom alone together since that one steamy kiss, and she knew he was remembering it too—could feel his eyes on hers as she fiddled with her hair in the mirror, finally daring to meet them with the safety of her back to him.

'You look—' A beat of a pause, and she watched as he walked a step nearer, close enough for her to witness a tiny swallow, the bob of his Adam's apple in his throat before he continued, 'You look beautiful.'

She always did, Vaughan thought, but tonight, despite the make-up, the glittering earrings and skilfully blow-dried hair, for the first time since they'd met she looked like the woman who had woken him so rudely—the woman who had spun into his office and into his life.

Her eyes were huge in her tiny face, tendrils of hair wisped around her face, and Vaughan tried to place just what it was that was different, what it was that reminded him so much of something. And then he got it. The smart business suits she'd worn since then had gone. Instead she was wearing clothing of her choice, and the sheer lilac was close to the shade of the top she had worn that first day he'd met her. That overtly feminine body was more visible now, without the harsh darts of her tailored suits, without the anonymous safety of muted greys. Her pearly shoulders were on display, and a teasing glimpse of her spinal cord, and his fingers bunched into a fist, fighting the urge to reach out and touch her.

He could see the swell of her bust in the mirror, the teasing movement of her unhindered bosom. The ruched top strained an erotic fraction with the rise and fall of her breathing—and if he'd wanted her before it didn't compare. He was hollow with lust now, could feel with total recall those full rosebud lips on his, the weight of her bosom in his hand. And he couldn't not touch her. Could no more just offer his arm to casually escort her than fly to the moon.

'We should go down.' Amelia's voice was slightly breathless. Her back was still to him, her eyes wide with apprehension in the mirror as only his head moved, bowing slowly.

He felt the shiver of reaction ripple through her as his lips met her shoulder, and he took a tiny slice of time, a fraction of what he couldn't have, inhaling her scent as his mouth parted over her soft skin before pulling away.

A touch, a tiny kiss on her shoulder, that was all it had been—yet Amelia knew it shouldn't have happened. She was angry at him for not playing by the rules, felt as if she'd been branded with a curious, erotic, almost possessive gesture she couldn't interpret. As if he'd sunk in his teeth, as if he'd left a mark, she could feel where he'd been, but she knew there was nothing visible to show for his touch. And as they headed downstairs, as they stood apart in the lift, made their way over to the cocktail lounge, still she could feel the weight of his lips where they'd made contact, spinning her into confusion all over again.

She wasn't sure which was worse—fighting the sexual tension, constantly being on high alert, or the safety of being with Vaughan when he was on his best behaviour. Since their lunch date, it was as if a light had been switched. Vaughan was polite, sometimes friendly, but always distant, treating her as he hadn't from the start.

As the journalist she was.

Until tonight.

Tonight she could feel the rules being rewritten. She felt like a pawn in one of Vaughan's games, moving at his will, her eyes constantly drawn to the master, acutely aware of him by her side,

'These are the auction items.' Clearly delighted by Vaughan's presence, Sam made his way over. 'And that fabulous holiday you donated is the cream of the crop. I hope you'll be pushing up the prices unashamedly for us.'

Vaughan didn't even deign to respond, just

shrugged his tense shoulders, taking two glasses of champagne and giving one to Amelia. His face broke into the widest of smiles as a couple waved cheerfully at him, and only the tiny roll of his eyes told her it was false. That almost conspiratorial gesture had her glowing, made her feel for a teasing glimpse as if she was on his side, as if they really were a couple.

'How's your piece going?' Vaughan attempted, fingering his collar, clearly wishing he was anywhere else but here.

'Good,' Amelia responded, glad at least something in her life was straightforward. Because sexual frustration had done wonders for her writing skills. Had given her permission to dwell on what she'd spurned. To legitimately focus on what she'd chosen not to have.

And because it was Vaughan her work was beautiful.

The intimate portrayal she'd been trying to achieve was coming to life beneath her fingers now. Somehow she was injecting his flashes of dry humour that softened the cruellest blows, capturing the enigmatic force of the man as he entered a room and intermingling it with the occasional glimpse of a different side—the active brain that kept him awake—divulging to her audience the softer side he usually chose not to reveal. And, despite what Paul said, Vaughan alone was quite simply enough to fill the pages. Amelia didn't need to name names, to foster attention, didn't need to add drama to a subject as enigmatic as he—there was no need for salacious gossip that wouldn't see the weekend out, and she'd take it to the line with her boss if she had to.

Watching him in action now, watching him working the room, glass in hand, haughty face occasionally softened with laugher, Amelia knew in a proud moment of realisation that she had made the right choice.

His beauty was timeless, and in turn so too would be her article.

If her career was on the line then that was okay—if her paper didn't want it then someone else surely would.

Vaughan had done nothing wrong—it wasn't his fault that she loved him.

'God, I hate these things,' he said, ages later, when Amelia had air-kissed more women than she could ever hope to remember and shaken hands with more ruddy-faced businessmen than she'd ever wanted to.

But Vaughan hadn't looked as if he'd hated it. On the contrary, he'd been a social wizard, listening intently to the most boring of conversations, laughing loudly at the most appalling jokes, yet he had still been true to himself, Amelia realized. On his best behaviour Vaughan might be, but not once had he come across as gushing.

'I wish they'd just bloody get on with the auction so I can call it a night.'

'It's for charity,' Amelia chided. 'As Sam keeps saying, think of the kids. I really think you should let me use this.'

'Don't—' Vaughan started, but there was no stopping Amelia now. Two cocktails and this amazing man at her side and Amelia was sure she could put the entire world to rights.

'It really is a good cause, Vaughan. And with the best will in the world one auction isn't going to deliver the equipment the ward needs. Surely a bit of publicity can only do you both some good?'

'Leave it, Amelia,' Vaughan warned, but the bit was between her teeth now and she refused to relent.

'No heart and flowers, I promise. But surely a mention is deserved. Sam reckons two lines in a newspaper could triple tonight's efforts.'

'You've been speaking to him?' One hand gripped her arm, the other wrapped firmly around his glass.

'Of course I've been speaking to him. These kids really need all the support you can give.'

'Just a couple of lines?' Vaughan checked. 'Maybe a brief description of the type of equipment they need?'

'Done!' Amelia responded, mentally pencilling it in—the perfect touch to the perfect article. But Vaughan's hand was still on her arm, his fingers still tight around her bare flesh. Wriggling free, she turned to him. 'Relax, for heaven's sake.'

'I am relaxed,' Vaughan hissed.

Sam was warming up the audience, reminding them all of the importance of the charity they were bidding for, while simultaneously urging them all to drink and be merry, clearly hoping a few cocktails might loosen their wallets. Beside her Vaughan stood stock-still, his body rigid with tension, a muscle pounding like a jackhammer in his cheek. Amelia just smiled wider.

'Oh, come on, Vaughan. If you hold that glass any

tighter it will shatter. You're going to be fine up there. Anyway, it's for a good cause, remember?'

'You really think that I'm worked up about this?' Incredulous eyes swung to hers, his head moving down to Amelia's slightly, ensuring only she could hear his words. 'You really think that I'm worried about taking the stage?'

Bewildered, she shrugged. 'Vaughan, if you don't want me to put this in the article you only have to say—'

'Amelia.' His tone was savage, and his hand was back in place on her arm, pulling her around to face him. 'Have you any idea how you look tonight?' He gave a mirthless laugh. 'I'm sure you do. Is that why you didn't wear a bra?'

Startled eyes met his, and she gave a tiny gasp in her throat as she stepped back, attempting to duck the onslaught. She was completely unprepared, and there was nowhere to go. The spotlight was beaming its way towards them, the trickle of applause building as Sam invited Vaughan Mason to take the floor.

But Vaughan wasn't going anywhere in a hurry. His features were severe in the white heat of the spotlight, his voice a threatening caress, his eyes dragging over her décolletage. She felt as if she were naked, her nipples sticking like thistles in her dress. So acute was his stare that she could almost feel the cool of his lips suckling them, feel the inappropriate stir of her own arousal as the room looked on—and surely they must know, surely they must see the pulse leaping between her legs, the twitching contractions of early arousal? If ever she had hated him it was at that moment, her angry, lust-loaded eyes glaring back at him, as she willed it to be over.

'Don't play with me, Amelia. Don't try and play games with the big boys, because as you know they don't always follow the rules.'

And he couldn't have cheapened her more, couldn't have made her feel more like a whore—as if she'd dressed deliberately provocatively to entice him, as if he hadn't come pounding on the door when she should have been getting ready. Worst of all, she had no choice but to take it, no choice but to force a smile as he took the microphone and with effortless ease worked the room, his clipped tones such a contrast to Sam's needy ones.

Yet it had the desired effect. Serious bidding was taking place, and she watched, burning with indignation yet dripping with lust, as bidding moved ever higher, as once again Vaughan succeeded where others would surely have failed.

Well, he wouldn't succeed with her.

The microphone was barely back in its stand, the small talk only just starting up again, as Amelia headed for the door, punching in the lift number, aching to get to her room, to scream into a pillow. But Vaughan was behind her, calling her back.

'It isn't finished yet.'

'Oh, but it is, Vaughan—for me, at least. You're so cocksure, so bloody arrogant, so certain all any woman wants is to sleep with you...' Her cheeks burnt with anger, but her lips were pale, so taut she could barely get the words out without hissing. 'I was right about you all along—you haven't changed a bit, you've just learnt to be more discreet.'

'What the hell are you going on about?'

'You think all you have to do is turn on the charm and I'll relent. You're so sure that everything is somehow engineered towards snaring the great Vaughan Mason! A woman doesn't wear a bra and you assume that it's for your benefit! My God, you really think the world revolves around you, don't you? Did it never enter your head that had you not needed help getting dressed then I might have had more time to get ready?'

'You've been flirting with me all night,' Vaughan insisted, but Amelia shook her head.

'*You* kissed *me*, Vaughan.' Her finger moved to the spot, the very spot, where his lips had scorched her flesh. 'You were the one who came uninvited into my room and stood and watched me getting ready. You were the one who kissed me. So don't you dare try and turn this onto me. Don't turn this around and make it so that it's me wanting you.'

She made to go, ready to run the last few steps back to her bedroom, painfully aware that another woman had had him today, had tasted him, adored him, determined not to relent. But his hand closed around her wrist like a vice, capturing her, swinging her around to face him in one fluid motion, confronting her with a fact they both knew to be true.

'But you do.'

His voice was thick with emotion, his hand looser now, and she could have left, could have walked away this very second. But instead she stood. 'You do,' he said for a second time, and she wished she had a solicitor present—someone to step in and call a halt to his line of questioning, to pull her out before she gave in, before she voiced a truth that could surely only sentence her. 'You've wanted me from the day you walked into my office. You've wanted me as much as I've wanted you. I know I've got a past, but…'

'Your past is a bit too recent for me to swallow!' Amelia retorted, and registered the tiny frown between his eyes. 'Who was she, Vaughan?' She choked the words out, hating herself for asking, but needing to know. 'Who was the woman who left your room this afternoon?'

She felt his hand tighten on her wrist, watched as he swallowed hard, a nervous dart in his eyes before finally they met hers.

'You have to trust me there…'

'Trust you!' An incredulous shrill laugh escaped her lips. 'Trust *you*?'

'Yes, me.' His voice was even, his eyes holding hers, imploring her. 'Trust me when I say that I cannot tell you now, Amelia, and believe me when I say that it's not what you're thinking.'

'I need to know who she is, Vaughan,' Amelia begged. 'You can't just ask me to trust you, to believe…'

'Because of what Taylor did?'

'Because I can't do this again, Vaughan.' She was sobbing now, consumed by her own arousal, terrified by her own weakness, knowing how close she was to relenting, to giving in, to backing him in the face of such appalling odds. 'I've been hurt before—believed someone when they said they'd mended their ways, that I was the only one…'

'But I have changed, Amelia,' he rasped. 'These past few months I've realised that I want more.'

'And what about this sudden change? What brought about this great epiphany?' Amelia asked furiously, but her anger was directed at herself, that she could even allow this discussion to continue, terrified of being dragged in a touch deeper, that she might believe his lies.

'A seven-year-old boy made me realise it was time to grow up!'

And something in his voice moved her. Something in the pain behind the hesitant words told her this was real.

'That's all I can tell you now, Amelia. All I can tell you without betraying a confidence I've sworn to keep.'

'It doesn't make sense…'

'It *can't* make sense while you're still a journalist contracted to do a piece on me,' Vaughan implored. 'I can't tell you any more than that.'

'And I can't just…'

He was kissing her cheeks, tiny butterfly kisses. His full lips soaked up her tears as they fell, and her words shuddered out of chattering lips.

'I can't…' Amelia gasped, her back against the wall, furious in denial. But she knew it was the flailing of a drowning woman. Skin on skin, his hands slid to her upper arms, and his lips mingled with tears as his words breezed past her cheeks, seared the tiny hairs in her ears, ripping apart her defences as he rasped his prosecution.

'You can.' One hand cupped her breast, the nub of his thumb grazing across her tender nipple. Her throat constricted, lust searing through her. 'You can.'

Yes!

She didn't say it, but her body was his affirmation, yielding towards him. As she dared to admit the truth mentally her mouth opened to speak—to say what, she didn't know. Beg a retraction, perhaps? Plead for mercy? But the tiny window of opportunity was open and he stormed right in, possessing her mouth with his, forcing her so hard against the hotel door she could feel the breath being squeezed out of her, mingling with his.

That first initial taste she'd craved like an addiction for days now was finally on her lips. Freeing her arms, she coiled them into his hair in a reflex action, fingers and nails burying into his thick jet-black hair. Pushing his full weight onto her, he confirmed her desire, catching her tongue with his, and if her own boldness surprised her, then Vaughan was already way ahead, his free hand slipping up the petticoat of her sequinned dress, moulding the soft flesh just above her stockings, capturing her groin for such a dizzy moment she could have come right there.

Shockingly unaware of their location, she let a tiny whimper of frustration escape as Vaughan's mouth paused. Somehow he opened the door. Wrapping her legs around his waist, he lifted her up and carried her inside to the bedroom. The soft mattress barely registered in her thoughts as he lowered her down onto the bed.

Allowing her not even a tiny second to acclimatize, he ripped the earth from beneath her, pushing up the sequinned hem of her dress, tearing at her panties, burying his face in her most intimate place. He danced her like a puppeteer, toying with the knot of tension deep inside her with each vivid stroke of his tongue. She could feel him everywhere, in her constricted throat, in her thighs, which convulsed as he stroked ever deeper, in her stomach, which contracted with the first twitches of her orgasm. A moan of pure lust and need ripped away from her as he leant back on his heels, leaving her moaning and twitching with unfilled desire—until she saw him.

Saw the sheer naked sex of him slowly undressing. She hated him for her exposure as she lay breathless on the bed, watching his teasing disrobing. Cufflinks that took for ever to remove, an impatient rip at the button she'd so nervously sewn, a pull at the tie that, if scissors had been handy, she'd have cut. She glimpsed the silver of his zipper, the beauty of his package as his boxers were lowered. His jutting arousal did it to her all over again. But need took over then, knees inside knees, his thighs deftly parting her thighs, the scratch of his legs against her skin, the delicious thrill of anticipation.

'This is what you want?'

Beyond the point of no return, still he gave her the option, still he offered her an out. But she didn't want it—couldn't even begin to fathom the consequences of saying no to such a basic need. Amelia just knew that she had to, wanted to, needed to see this through to its delicious end, board this rollercoaster ride of passion. Yes, it was terrifying, exhilarating and dangerous, and yet it was something she simply had to do.

Her thighs dragged him in as his impatient hands pushed her dress up around her waist. Cupping her buttocks with his hands, eyes closing, he stabbed an entrance, thrusting deep inside her warmth. And she revelled in the delicious friction of him gliding inside her, came alive in his arms, dancing to his tune with a beat of her own now. Ecstasy was a mere breath away, a rush of heat galloping along her spine, flooding her neck, and her whole body aligned as he spilled inside her, the needy gasp escaping hushed by the salt warmth of his shoulder in her mouth. She sucked the flesh beneath her lips, capturing his manhood deep within, holding him tight, capturing the final throes of his orgasm with the intensity of her own. As her grip on his shoulder softened, the sheer force of emotion that had catapulted her imploded within, tears that had always been there but never been shed springing forth as still he held her.

'No regrets?'

Minutes perhaps hours later, the room came into focus, and she touched her bruised heart, waited for the appalling sting of reality, for the fingers of regret to start creeping in. But Vaughan's navy eyes were still adoring her, his body next to hers. The most exhilarating, breathtaking ride of her life had come slowly to a halt, and all Amelia knew was that she didn't ever want to get off, wanted to keep going, over and over again.

'None.' Amelia smiled back at Vaughan. 'Except for the fact I didn't take my make-up off.' Shifting herself onto her back she smiled into the darkness. 'That's a mortal sin, by the way.'

'So is falling asleep fully clothed.' His hand was toying with her zip, parting the flimsy fabric that ran along the curve of her side and dragging it down in a move that could only be translated as provocative. Kissing the hollow of her waist, he took his time at the curve of her buttocks, wriggling the sheer fabric down around her ankles before focusing on her shoes. 'And falling asleep in your shoes, young lady, is positively indecent.'

She knew he was waiting for her to laugh, knew as he looked up that he was expecting a smile. She could see the tiny frown on his brow as he sensed her distraction. 'What's wrong, Amelia?'

'Nothing.' Rolling into a pillow, she stared at the curtain. 'Nothing,' she said again, hoping for more conviction this time. But Vaughan wasn't to be fooled, and the concern in his voice matched hers as he spoke into the darkness.

'You're not on the Pill, are you?'

'No.'

A hundred questions shrilled in her brain. How could they have been so stupid? for one. It was the twenty-first century, for heaven's sake. There were condoms by the bed, courtesy of the hotel. It was beyond stupid not to be careful, but nothing, *nothing* prepared her for the tension that filled the body beside her, the slow hiss of air as he breathed slowly out.

'We have to do something. You have to take something. You *cannot* get pregnant.'

'Vaughan?' Questioning eyes turned to his. She was angry enough with herself at her own stupidity, but Vaughan's reaction wasn't exactly helping matters.

'There's a pill—the seventy-two-hour pill,' Vaughan said urgently. 'I can ring down for a doctor. Now.'

'We've still got seventy-one hours left!' It wasn't a joke exactly, merely an attempt to defuse the situation. She was scarcely able to believe what she was witnessing now—Vaughan Mason, completely perturbed, hands raking through his hair, wrestling with demons of his own that Amelia couldn't cope with right now. 'Vaughan, we made a mistake—a stupid mistake…'

'You're telling me…'

And suddenly she was angry. Angry and humiliated. He was acting as if she had a shotgun wedged under the pillow, as if she'd forced the night's events upon them, had somehow planned all this. But, seeing his anguished face, sensing something deeper was happening here, Amelia realised now probably wasn't the time to point out that it took two to tango, that the mistake had been as much his as hers.

'You're overreacting—' she started, but that only inflamed him more.

'Amelia, you don't understand. Trust me on this—you just cannot be pregnant…'

'Oh, but I think I do understand.' The air-conditioning must be up too high, because suddenly she was shivering, the intimacy they had shared slipping away like sand through her fingers. 'Trust you?' She shook her head angrily. 'I'm getting a little bit tired of being asked to trust you, Vaughan. In fact I'm starting to think you're treating me as some sort of—'

'Amelia,' Vaughan broke in icily. 'You're not the only one being asked to trust here. Might I remind you that you're a journalist? That's the entire bloody reason we're together, after all. You could be sleeping with me just to get a better slant on your story for all I know…'

And it was just too close to the mark, just too appallingly reminiscent of the innuendoes that had tarnished her reputation six months ago. Levering herself off the bed, Amelia searched for her dress, pulled it over her trembling body with her back firmly to him, attempted dignity in the face of utter humiliation. 'I'm not pregnant, Vaughan, so you don't have to worry. My period is due tomorrow, which means the chances of me getting pregnant are slim. Does that make you happy? What just took place wasn't about making babies but about making love—at least it was for me.'

'Don't go.'

Her hand was on the door; her instinct was to leave. The vileness of his accusation, the horror in his voice at the possible consequences of their actions had sounded a church's worth of alarm bells for Amelia, but almost instantly he quelled them, reverting in a second back to the man she was starting to know. He followed her to the door and pulled her tense body beside him, working her taut shoulders as he buried his face in her hair and whispered a heartfelt apology in her ear, leading her back to the bed.

'I'm sorry, Amelia.' His voice was pure anguish. 'I'm overreacting. It's just…' His voice petered out, but Amelia wanted more, still reeling from the abrupt change in him.

'Just what, Vaughan?' Amelia asked. 'You're talking as if I set out to trap you, as if—'

'No.' Instantly he refuted her accusation and pulled her back down to lie beside him. 'I'm angry with myself, not you. Angry with myself that I didn't stop and think.'

'It's called emotion, Vaughan. People don't always stop and think before they act. As you've said, this is the bedroom, not the boardroom. You don't always go in prepared.' He nodded at her explanation, pulled her in just a little bit tighter, yet she sensed his distraction, could almost feel his mind whirring as they lay staring into the darkness.

'Have you sent your article?'

Frowning into his chest, she waited for him to elaborate, pulling away when he didn't and propping herself up on her elbow, staring down at him. 'What's that got to do with anything?'

'I just want to know, that's all.'

'No, it hasn't gone.' Her words whistled through tight lips. 'Vaughan, what am I missing here? Are you worried I'm going to say something? That what took place tonight might change what I write?'

'Of course not.' And like the wind he changed

again—the pensive mood gone, the dynamic man back in her arms again. 'But if you do, remember to write just how damn good I am.'

She did all the right things—laughed at his joke, even got fully undressed again and climbed right in beside him, curving herself as he spooned in behind her, relishing the delicious feel of his hand cupping her stomach, the rhythmic rise and fall of his breathing. Yet still Amelia frowned into the darkness, still she didn't feel entirely comforted.

Something had happened a moment ago that she didn't understand. She had witnessed a side to him she truly couldn't fathom.

There was something big that Vaughan was holding back.

CHAPTER SEVEN

'YOU can break the news of the motor deal.'

Blinking as she opened her eyes, Amelia attempted to focus. Sun streamed in through open curtains, accentuating the chaos of the rumpled bed, her shoes on the floor, her dress as crumpled as a dishrag. But it didn't matter a jot, because sitting on the bed beside her, immaculate in a sharp suit and smiling down at her, was the one thing that made waking up a sheer, indisputable pleasure.

'What happened to good morning?' Stretching like a cat, she caught the first delicious aroma of morning coffee, the absolute perfect touch to the perfect awakening. Scarcely able to fathom that not only had she made love to him, but also she didn't for a second regret it, she said, 'Is that for me?' Reaching over, she took a grateful sip, aware all the while of his eyes smiling down at her, not remotely self-conscious, feeling as beautiful as the eyes that adored her. 'How long have you been up?'

'An hour. I've been in the lounge suite, chatting to Mr Cheng.'

'Do you always put on a suit to talk on the phone?' Amelia teased, but of course Vaughan always had an answer.

'It was a video conference. I didn't think he'd appreciate the sight of me in my bathrobe.'

'More fool him, then.' Amelia smiled, her forehead puckering as she recalled the news she had woken to. 'I can break it?'

'Yep.' Vaughan smiled as the penny dropped. 'Write that you have it on reliable authority that the deal is going to be formally announced on Monday.'

'But—'

'No buts,' Vaughan interrupted. 'I've spoken to Mr Cheng and he's more than happy to let some details out before the announcement. We both agree we'd rather it came from someone we know.'

'Trust, even?'

'Yeah.' Vaughan smiled as if he'd just discovered the word. 'That too.'

'You don't need to do this,' Amelia said, her voice suddenly serious. 'I've already told Paul that I'm going with the original article. I'm more than happy to stand by my decision and weather the consequences.'

'Well, you don't have to.' Vaughan squeezed her thigh through the sheet, 'This way you both win. You get to write what you want, and Paul gets the first sniff at the story—which will buy you some time to properly make up your mind.'

'I really can have it all.' Her hand reached up to his face, capturing that delicious sculptured cheek in her palm, feeling the soft scratch of his chin. Gently she guided his face in towards hers, enjoying the feel of a more leisurely kiss this time. The urgency had gone but the passion was deeper now, the giddy, insatiable lust that had spun them into the bedroom replaced with something just as exhilarating—a cavernous journey of emotion patiently awaiting their exploration, the thrill of peeling back the layers together, the silent promise of all tomorrow might hold.

'I have to go.'

Grumbling as he pulled away, Amelia lay back on the pillow.

'Where?' Seeing the dart in his eyes, Amelia held her breath. A single word had spilled from her lips, and her question had been entirely innocent, but something in Vaughan's stance told her she'd hit a nerve. 'You don't have to answer that,' she said quickly, swallowing back the hurt. But Vaughan saw through her defences.

'I want to tell you, Amelia, believe me. But I can't just yet.'

'Because you don't trust me?'

'No,' Vaughan responded immediately. 'Because this particular secret is not mine to reveal. You're the one who's going to have to trust me—for a little while longer anyway. I need to sort a few things out today. I need to run something by…' He paused for a beat. 'I need to speak to someone who matters, Amelia, and I can't do it with you there. Can you try and understand?'

She gave a brave nod, completely none the wiser but determined to trust him.

'And you, young lady—' Vaughan smiled '—have to write your article. What time's it due in?'

'Two—I thought I'd nearly finished and could spend the morning shopping, but, given what you've just told me about the motor deal I'd better drink this coffee and get writing. Paul was very clear that he wouldn't give me an extension.'

'How about a drink at the bar around three, then?' Vaughan suggested. 'Like I said, I've got a few things that need taking care of, but I should be finished by then and I promise then we can talk. Really talk,' he added, with feeling.

'Vaughan…' He was making to go, but her hand pulled him back, capturing the arm of his suit, and as his questioning gaze tried to meet her eyes she stared instead at her fingers, shy at what she was about to say, yet knowing she had to. 'What you said last night about…' A tiny nervous swallow halted her words and Vaughan took that moment to move in.

'The morning-after pill?' Vaughan checked

'If I don't get my period…'

'Amelia…' His voice was soft, the uptight man she had witnessed last night gone, seemingly a momentary lapse, as he took her hand and finally said the right thing. 'I was out of line last night. But please believe me when I say it was with good reason.' He glanced reluctantly at his watch. 'We'll talk this afternoon properly, but in the meantime, please, no doctors, no pills. Just hear what I have to say first.'

Even the clock ticking by at a rate of knots didn't darken the delicious day. Fashioning the piece Paul so desperately wanted was easy now, with Vaughan's consent. Yet she refused to let her feelings mar her objectivity, and she carefully outlined the potential pitfalls as well as celebrating the deal. The left side of her brain enjoyed the intellectual challenge as she rediscovered the passion that had initially brought her into journalism.

And maybe, just maybe, Vaughan was right. Why couldn't she keep her feet in both camps? Why did concentrating on one mean that she had to give up the other?

Maybe she really could have it all.

There was no stress headache as she filled up her bath this Friday. No anxious pangs, no superstitious routines firmly in place. Just a reckless feeling of exhilaration as she e-mailed her article. Slipping into the bath, she had no desire for retrieval, no surge of anxiety about commas to add or exclamation marks she might have missed—her work was good and Amelia knew it. Knew that the hard slog was over, that finally she'd made it, and could just lie back in the soapy water and allow that nagging right side of her brain to finally let rip, to concentrate on the one thing in her life that right now demanded her sole attention— the man who very soon would be waiting for her downstairs.

CHAPTER EIGHT

'MISS JACOBS?'

The smiling face was familiar, but Amelia took a moment to place it. Already onto her second glass of champagne, she had long since grown tired of staring expectantly towards the foyer, tired of the slightly curious stares of the hotel staff as she waited for Vaughan to join her, his empty glass on the table beside the bottle she'd ordered.

'Katy Vale!' Placing the face, Amelia gestured to the empty seat in front of her, but from the dismissive way she shook her head, clearly Vaughan's PA had other places she needed to be. 'What can I do for you?'

'I've got a message from Vaughan—something came up; he's not going to be able to meet you.'

Amelia waited for further explanation—the offer of an apology, even—but apparently Katy had said all she was going to. Already she was making to go, clearly satisfied that her message was delivered. But an hour and a half of sitting alone in the hotel bar nursing a lonely glass of champagne had Amelia's patience hanging by a thread.

'Did he say anything else?' Watching as the woman slowly turned, her eyes taking in the champagne bottle, the empty chair and glass, Amelia felt her cheeks darken. She cleared her throat to ensure her next sentence would be delivered in slightly less needy tones.

'Something came up.' Katy raised her palms to the ceiling. 'You know what Vaughan's like.'

Only she didn't.

The Vaughan who had sat on her bed this morning would no more have stood her up so coldly than fly to the moon—and yet, Amelia reminded herself, the Vaughan she'd glimpsed last night, the Vaughan she'd read about over the years, was more than capable of sending his PA to terminate things.

'Is there anything I can help you with?' Katy offered, her voice bordering on sympathetic as Amelia attempted a dignified shake of her head. 'Frankly, I'm surprised you're still here. I got the impression from Vaughan that your article was already in. Was there something you wanted to double check? I'm pretty well versed on everything…'

But Amelia wasn't listening. Her attention had been drawn to the foyer and, perhaps realising she'd lost her audience, Katy turned around too, following Amelia's gaze, watching in knowing silence as Vaughan entered the lobby.

As Amelia's world literally fell apart.

His hair for once was tousled, his tie loosened, white cotton shirtsleeves casually rolled up. But worse, far worse, was the fact he wasn't wearing his jacket. Instead it was draped around the shoulders of the beautiful woman Amelia had seen in the corridor yesterday. Her dark exotic features mocked Amelia a thousand times over, her tiny fragile body, her legs surely too thin to hold her up. But what did it matter when Vaughan was practically carrying her, one arm possessively draped around her shoulders, guiding her towards the lift?

Amelia's mind flailed for a reasonable explanation, begged, despite the blatant evidence, that perhaps she'd got it wrong. But as they reached the lift doors and Vaughan dragged his feminine parcel towards him, buried his face in her hair and held her tight, not even Amelia could attempt an excuse in the face of such overwhelming odds.

'Your article is in.' Katy's voice had a slightly bitchy ring, and eyes way too knowing for such a pretty face flashed in triumph or malice as Amelia slowly nodded. 'Then it would seem, Miss Jacobs, that your allotted time slot is over.'

A luxurious five-star hotel might have appeared the best place in the world to lick her wounds, but lying on the counterpane, too mentally and physically exhausted to climb into bed, Amelia stared at the screensaver on her computer, agonisingly aware of what was surely going on next door, but too raw, too ashamed and utterly too humiliated to interrupt—to barge her way in and demand an explanation when she already had one.

Her allocated time slot was over—Vaughan Mason had already moved on.

Why had she expected anything more? Vaughan had promised her precisely nothing, save a drink in the bar and a chance to talk.

What a fool to think she could have held him for more than a moment. What reckless thoughts had possessed her to believe for a moment that she alone could be enough to tame him?

Reliable, dependable—boring, perhaps. Even her period came on time. The low heavy thud hit her, just as she'd told Vaughan it would, and the dull, aching feeling in the pit of her stomach was painfully familiar. She felt the sting of nausea as she dragged her tired body out of the bathroom in response to the knocking on the door, even managing a wan smile at the cheerful face of the housekeeper as she bustled into the room.

Amelia wandered into the corridor, agony etched on agony as she heard low murmurs behind Vaughan's closed door, and the green 'Do Not Disturb' sign he'd hung blurred through tear-filled eyes.

She'd rather die than let him see her tears, Amelia decided; would rather walk away a bitch than a loser.

An idea was forming in her mind, growing in momentum as she strode down the corridor, took the lift to the lobby and walked out into the balmy evening sun. Call it determination, or self-preservation perhaps, but she'd been here before, just six months ago, had stood weeping at a hotel door for the first and very last time, and there was no way she was going to go there again.

Ever.

CHAPTER NINE

'VAUGHAN!'

As he opened the door she got her greeting in first, smiled an efficient smile at his scowling frown.

Prepared for the worst speech of her life.

'I'm sorry to disturb you.' She gestured to the sign on his door, prayed that the foundation she'd plastered on was really as good as it said in the adverts, that her burning cheeks and reddened nose weren't somehow peeping through. 'It's just that I need a quick word.'

'Amelia.' She could see his distraction, sense his obvious discomfort. He had one hand firmly on the door, careful not to allow it to open further, but even a mahogany door between them wasn't quite enough to drown out the unmistakable noise of a shower running in the background. 'I'm sorry about before. Did you get my message?' His voice was deliberately low, presumably so not to alert his companion to this annoying distraction, and at that moment Amelia hated him with a violence that shocked even herself. Loathed him for the degradation that suffused her.

She'd trusted him.

Trusted him with the most painful part of her life. And he'd chewed it up whole and spat it in her face, prostituted her with a pay-off—an article she hadn't, in the end, even particularly wanted.

For a small moment she was tempted to drag out the torture, to barge into his room and confront the woman she knew was in there, to force him to admit what Amelia already knew. But she couldn't bring herself to suffer the indignity of being proved right, to choke back tears as he humiliated her all over again.

If she were even to attempt a retreat with her dignity apparently intact, somehow she had to do this—somehow she had to look him in the eye and deliver the biggest lie of her life.

'This isn't a great time for me, Amelia. Something unexpected came up…' His voice was low and urgent, and again he briefly checked over his shoulder. 'Can we maybe catch up later?'

'Later is no good for me, Vaughan,' Amelia responded firmly, registering the dart of confusion in his eyes at her clipped, assured voice. 'The office just called. They need me to head back to Sydney—something big just came up.'

'And you have to go right now?'

'Right now,' Amelia confirmed, a brittle smile flashing on her face as Vaughan briefly eyed the bulging suitcase on the floor beside her before turning his gaze back to her. 'I just stopped by to say goodbye.'

'Then call me when you get back to your home—' Vaughan started, and a frown formed between his eyes as Amelia shook her head.

'Look, Vaughan, like I said, something big just came up. I could be stuck in the office for hours. I might even have to go on assignment. So I've no idea when I'm going to get back.' Glancing down at her watch, she gave what she hoped was a convincing wince. 'I'd better rush if I'm going to get my flight.'

Vaughan's frown deepened as Amelia shook her head and somehow managed a kind but slightly patronising smile.

'Let's not go making promises we can't keep. Let's not pretend that last night was anything more than…' She allowed him a tiny pause, a brief moment to let it sink in, because it wouldn't be easy for a man like Vaughan to fathom that a woman was actually rejecting him, Amelia realised. Like Taylor, he was completely used to getting his own way—flashing a winning smile and instantly being forgiven. But, as much as Taylor's infidelity had hurt, Vaughan's abuse of her trust had cut her to the core, shredded every fibre of her faith; yet somehow from agony came strength; somehow the torture of his betrayal allowed her to draw on an inner reserve, to look him in the eye and lie outright.

'It was business, Vaughan.'

He shook his head in vehement denial, the colour draining out of his already ashen face. His face quilted with raw emotion and, forgetting the door he held, he instinctively reached out for her, grabbing her upper arm, shaking her, his eyes imploring her to take back what she had just said.

'That was never business. What we had last night was way more than that, and you know it, Amelia.' His voice was rising now. A housekeeper passing with her trolley looked over in concern, and Amelia watched as Vaughan struggled to hold it together, dropping her arm from his vice-like grip, swallowing down hard to rid his voice of coarse emotion. 'That wasn't just business.'

'No, Vaughan, you're right.' She gave a small shrug and, bending over, picked up her case. 'It was pleasurable too. Unlike yourself, I can actually manage to mix the two.'

'So that's it?' Bewildered, he shook his head, and Amelia knew she'd thrown him into confusion, could see the utter abhorrence in his eyes that a woman could so easily turn the tables on him. 'You were using me?'

'We were using each other, Vaughan,' Amelia explained, apparently patiently, though her heart was hammering in her chest, bile rising in her throat as she cheapened herself to his level. But not for a second did she reveal it, standing not very tall, but somehow proud as Vaughan received a small taste of the medicine that over the years he'd so regularly given out. 'I've got the story I wanted and you've got the press on your side—for now, at least.'

It gave her the first stab of pleasure she'd felt since seeing him in the foyer, a tiny hint of bitter joy in reprisal, and it stirred her on to twist the knife in its final turn.

'It's been *nice*, Vaughan.'

Offering her hand, she wondered if he'd take it, wondered if he'd recover his ego quickly enough to attempt the upper hand. But Vaughan was clearly struggling, raking his hand through his hair, his breath coming loud and harsh as he turned to the door that had slammed behind him. For a tiny instant Amelia actually felt sorry for him, watching this dignified, proud man rummaging in his pockets for the swipe card, then standing back as the housekeeper who had been hovering moved to let him in, then stepped back again as the door opened of its own accord.

'What's going on?'

Dark hair still wet from the shower spilled down over olive shoulders, and the face devoid of make-up was nothing short of exquisite. Somehow Amelia processed these facts. Somehow she managed to stand as gravity lost its pull. Those exotic eyes she had viewed from a distance in the foyer were even more beautiful close up, with flecks of gold in their feline depths as she slowly took in the scene, then looked up to Vaughan, demanding an explanation.

'Is there a problem?'

If this woman couldn't work it out for herself then Amelia wasn't going to enlighten her—which maybe went against the grain of sisterhood, but frankly, at that moment in time, Amelia didn't care.

'There's no problem, Liza.' Vaughan offered a reassuring smile. 'Amelia's just a journalist, sniffing around for a story.' Navy eyes that had once adored her stared at her now with disgust. 'Isn't that right?'

'But what does she want?' Liza demanded, wary eyes slanting more suspiciously now—only not at Vaughan, but directly at Amelia. 'Don't you lot have any respect for other people's privacy? There's a "Do Not Disturb" sign on the door—how dare you just intrude...?'

'It's okay, Liza.' His voice was supremely gentle as he guided her back inside—an utter contrast to the black look of hatred he was shooting at Amelia. 'It's nothing for you to worry about; nothing at all.'

Slamming the door in her face, he left her standing. And despite what he'd done, despite the pain he'd caused, somehow he'd still managed to win. Somehow he'd managed to turn the tables on her. His rejection, his outright abhorrence towards her, was such a far cry from anything she could have imagined. The pain in his eyes, the lack of dignity in his defeat…

In one fell swoop he'd soured her tiny taste of victory—and worst of all, Amelia realised as she stood there, shocked and reeling, had been the softness in his voice when he'd spoken to Liza. The protectiveness of his gestures had cut her to the core.

It was jealousy that was choking her as she gathered up her case and stumbled to the lift, jealousy seeping from every pore, every fibre in her body, as she hobbled like a wounded animal along the long, lonely corridor.

Vaughan Mason was a bare-faced liar, a cruel, vindictive bastard, and yet…

Punching the lift button, leaning back against the cool glass mirrors, finally she gave in to the tears that would surely choke her…

She wanted it to be her.

Wanted Vaughan to be wrapping his arms around her. Wanted Vaughan shooing away the world for her when it all got too close.

Vaughan Mason was the man she truly loved.

CHAPTER TEN

'Sorry, there's absolutely nothing.' The ground stewardess tapped away at her computer one more time for luck. 'I'm afraid Friday night out of Melbourne is possibly the worst time to get a cancellation. There's nothing till the red-eye tomorrow at six a.m.'

'That's fine.' Amelia ran a tired hand through her hair. 'If you can book me on that, it would be great.'

Perhaps the stewardess had expected a wail of protest, a demand to see her supervisor, because when Amelia meekly accepted she offered her first smile. 'You can check your luggage in now, if you like.' As she snapped a label around Amelia's case, her smile moved to sympathetic. 'Do you want me to call the airport hotel? See if I can get you a room?'

Amelia shook her head. 'I'll just wait in the terminal.'

And she would. Because time seemed to have taken on no meaning now. There was no point paying for a bed she surely wouldn't use, and—bizarrely—she didn't want today to be over. Didn't want to close her eyes on a day that had started so perfectly and ended in disaster. Didn't want to go to sleep tonight because that would mean she'd have to wake up tomorrow, wake up and move on to the next phase of her life.

And right now she wasn't ready to face her grief alone.

But sitting at a café, drinking coffee after coffee, listening to the piped music, Amelia decided that Melbourne Airport was perhaps the loneliest place she'd ever been.

Hordes of people milled around, with trolleys clipping ankles, children dodging parents, reunited couples embracing, tearful lovers parting, and she watched it all. Occasionally she headed outside to stand in the warm night air, staring at the illuminated glass tunnel that led towards the terminals, remembering walking along it with Vaughan at the start of their adventure, remembering how good her life had been the last time she'd been there—the broad set of his shoulders as she'd clipped along behind, laughing at some throwaway comment Vaughan had made. She was scarcely able to comprehend that it had been just a few short days he had been in her world; that a man she had known for such a short space of time could be etched on her heart for ever.

Thought she had known, Amelia corrected, shaking her head as an anxious flyer attempted to cadge a light for his final cigarette before boarding.

Her pensive mood shifted slightly then, the inner reserve that had seen her through her degree, helped her forge her way in the cut-throat world of journalism, revealing just a tiny glimpse of the silver lining around the blackest cloud to enter her life.

She'd be okay. Amelia knew that deep down— knew that she deserved better than Vaughan Mason was prepared to give. She'd been right in what she'd said to Vaughan at the restaurant—she wanted it all, and she wouldn't settle for less.

The bundles of early editions outside the closed newsagent's had Amelia stopping in her tracks, and it would have taken a will of iron to move on and not take one. This was her work, after all. It was her name beside the headline.

What Price a Heart?

Frowning, Amelia glanced up at the newsagent, shutters firmly down, but that was the least of her problems. The headline didn't make sense. Okay, she hadn't sat typing wearing the rose-coloured glasses of first love, but she certainly hadn't portrayed Vaughan as ruthless.

Nothing in her article had portrayed him as heartless.

She could see the curious looks of a cleaner as, intending to pay in the morning, she ripped open the plastic bundle and pulled out a newspaper, intending to take it over to a table and sit down and read.

She didn't even make it one step.

The fragile beauty of Liza was captured in a photo as she unfolded the paper. Vaughan's arm was protectively around her, just as she had witnessed back at the hotel, but the caption beneath screamed words she had never even thought of, shaming her to the very core as somehow she read on.

Mason comforts his sister-in-law Liza.

Horrified, her eyes widened as she read the article, trying to drag in a lungful of air as her breathing came shallow and fast, her pulse pounded rapidly in her temples. Though Amelia had never had a panic attack this was as close to one as she ever wanted to come— she was drenched, literally drenched in revulsion as she read tomorrow's news, and the only thing that stopped her from collapsing, stopped her knees literally buckling beneath her, was the knowledge that she had to forewarn Vaughan—somehow tell him how appallingly he'd been treated, try and get him to understand that even though her name was on the article she'd played no part in this.

She just made it to the washroom in time.

She retched over and over at the mere thought of the damage that had been done. Everything made sense now, but she knew—*knew*—that never in a million years would Vaughan understand that she hadn't wittingly played a part in this.

The taxi ride was hell. Every light to the city was red as the yellow cab bumped through the empty streets. The taxi driver, oblivious to her despair, attempted idle chit-chat, but she couldn't even feign politeness, just stared out of the window as the city closed in. The beauty of Collins Street in the early hours of morning had zero impact, the fairy lights adorning the trees that lined the streets, the impressive entrance to the hotel barely registered in her mind— just the knowledge that in a few short minutes she had to face him.

Only as she reached his door did it strike her that he mightn't even be there, or, worse still, that perhaps

Liza might be with him. The thought of facing her, of facing them both together, of watching their reaction as they read the paper she held in her trembling hands assassinated Amelia as she summoned the courage to knock on the door.

'What the hell—' Dressed in dark boxers, his hair tousled from sleep, his eyes squinting to focus, never had he looked more desirable—or more completely unreachable.

'I need to talk to you,' Amelia choked, but Vaughan was already closing the door.

'Well, I don't want to listen.' Dismissing her, Vaughan shook his head, but as she held up the paper the closing door stilled, his eyes catching the headline just as Amelia's had.

He ripped the paper from her and headed inside, leaving her to walk in uninvited and watch as he sat on the edge of the bed, shoulders slumping as he read on. She let him do it in silence, knew that the time for excuses could only come when Vaughan was fully armed with the facts.

'Bitch.' He whistled the word out through taut pale lips, his eyes damning her to hell as he hit her with the full weight of his blistering stare. And even though it was agony to receive it, Amelia knew that from where Vaughan sat she deserved every last crumb of his contempt.

'I didn't know.' Her voice was a pale whisper, her teeth chattering so violently she could barely get the words out.

'That's not what it says here.' His voice was like ice. 'In fact,' he sneered, 'it says in black and white

''What Price a Heart'', by Carter Jenkins and Amelia Jacobs.'

'I didn't know about your nephew.' Tears were coursing down her cheeks but she didn't even notice, didn't even attempt to wipe them away. 'I didn't know anything, Vaughan, I swear.'

'Bull!' he cracked. 'You're asking me to believe that you had no idea the paper was planning this?'

'No!' She screamed her denial. 'I knew they had a story but I had no idea they were planning this! Vaughan, I thought Liza was your girlfriend. I was so jealous when I saw you with her that I decided to beat you to it—decided to pretend that our night had all just been about business. I didn't know your nephew had cystic fibrosis. God, I didn't even know you had a nephew, let alone that he was waiting for a heart-lung transplant...'

'Everybody knows now.' The despair in his eyes, the chasm of his pain, was palpable. 'They're insinuating that I'm trying to *buy* him treatment.' His voice was a raw whisper, but it did nothing to veil the hatred behind it. 'They're insinuating that I'm waving money so that he can jump the queue!'

'They're not going to deny him care on the strength of this,' Amelia begged, but Vaughan just shook his head.

'They're going to have to dot every ''i'' and cross every ''t'' now—to ensure they're seen to do the right thing—instead of going with their gut instinct. And that is that he needs it—soon. That's why Liza was here, Amelia, to tell me that Jamie's nearing the end, that without a transplant he's going to die...'

And far worse than his rage and anger was watching this proud, commanding man literally crumple before her, head in hands, every muscle in his shoulders strung with tension, fists balling into his temples as he processed the full horror of what he had just learnt.

His animosity was gone as he spoke on, but Amelia wasn't blind enough to believe it was over. He was merely voicing his fears. The fact that she was there was almost immaterial now.

'I've bent over backwards to ensure this didn't get out—knew that if the papers got hold of it somehow they'd twist it.' He gave a low, mirthless laugh. 'And the saddest part of it all is that I couldn't buy him a heart and lungs if I tried. Believe me, I've wanted to—I'd lose it all without even a hint of regret if I could give Jamie this chance. But even all my money, all my power, counts for nothing against the doctors. They deal with it every day, make choices no one else can, and not for a moment does money come into it. You didn't write that did you?' His anger was coming back now, disgust sneering on his face as he looked up to her. 'Just layered innuendo on innuendo, half truths combined with fact.'

'That wasn't me.'

'Well, that's not what it says here, Amelia.' Punching the paper away with his hand, he hurled it across the room, his naked anger confronting her. 'I quote: "handing a white envelope over to one of the hospital's directors in a secluded Melbourne restaurant…" It was a prize, for God's sake. A holiday prize I didn't even want my name put to, Amelia. You've made it sound like a bribe.'

'Carter was there…' Amelia gulped. Things were making more sense with hindsight.

'You saw him?'

Amelia nodded, her eyes riddled with guilt by association, and knew that she was going down for the third time—knew that nothing she could say would convince him she hadn't known what the paper was planning.

Knew that she'd lost him.

Vaughan was right. The article had her name on it. Fact and innuendo was a dangerous blend indeed, and Paul had been careful, because from Amelia's one look through the newspaper there wasn't a single lie. Her carefully crafted words were interlaced with Carter's insinuations. Overtones of corruption sounded in every paragraph, paling everything else into insignificance. Even the motor deal announcement barely merited a mention.

If ever she'd been ashamed of her profession it was then.

'I trusted you.' She noticed the past tense of his words and it lacerated her. 'I even thought I loved you, Amelia. I went to the hospital today to speak to Liza, to ask her if I could tell you about Jamie. To tell her that I'd met this amazing woman who just happened to be a journalist, that for once I was sure I'd got it right. What a fool!'

Ignoring his last line, Amelia probed gently, filled with regret for all she had done, the love she had thrown away, but needing to hear how close she had come to realising her dream. 'What did she say?'

'I didn't get to tell her.' Vaughan's face hardened,

yet she could see the pain behind it, see his knuckles whitening as he clenched his fists together in an effort to hold things back. 'Jamie's condition had deteriorated overnight—nothing definable, of course, nothing the doctors can put their fingers on or qualify to the press as reasons for moving him to the top of the transplant list. So I doubt it will happen now.' He stared at her paling face, rammed in the knife just a touch further, shaming her all over again. 'I brought Liza back here for a break, so she could have a shower and bawl her eyes out away from her son, to give her a chance to admit her terror. It didn't seem the right time to talk about my love-life.' His head was in his hands again, and he was speaking more to himself than to her. 'Or appalling lack of it.'

'I'll go.'

Her voice was a mere croak and Vaughan looked up briefly, pulling his head out of his hands just long enough to loathe her.

'Why not? After all, you got what you came for.'

CHAPTER ELEVEN

It FELT as if she were coming home after a funeral, mourning the loss of what she'd so recently had. And her apartment seemed steeped in a life that was divided into two—before and after Vaughan.

Before, when things like bath oils had mattered, when horoscopes had held promises, when she'd thought she had it tough, had been so naïve as to think that Taylor's infidelity was as low as life went.

How naïve, how pathetically naïve to think then that she had known pain. The loss she had felt at the end of her relationship with Taylor didn't even compare to the raw grief that held her in its vice-like grip now.

The waxy pink petals of the orchids Vaughan had sent her were the first thing to catch her eye, and she couldn't help but realise that they had lasted longer than them, and there wasn't a single thing she could do.

'I guess I just fell in love,' Amelia whispered, scarcely able to comprehend that something so beautiful could hurt so much.

And was it worth the pain?

She could almost hear Vaughan asking the question and remembered that first night at the hotel, standing on tired, aching feet at the threshold of the love affair of a lifetime, thought of her bruised, raw, shredded heart. Without hesitation she nodded into the lonely room.

'Absolutely.'

She knew he'd never forgive her, knew her time with Vaughan was over, yet she ached to put things right, to somehow repair some of the damage she'd unwittingly inflicted. But at every turn she was thwarted. Her angry demands for a retraction were met with an incredulous laugh from Paul, who was completely unable to comprehend why she wasn't wallowing in the glory of it all.

Hours dragged into days, her anger giving way to lethargy, and it was a supreme effort just to lever herself off the couch to answer the door. Flowers were being delivered, even a bottle of champagne, and her telephone was constantly ringing with messages of congratulations. Even her father, for the first time, was proud of his daughter's work.

But the one person she wanted to see, the one person she wanted to hear from, kept a dignified silence.

No outburst of temper on the six o'clock news, just the stern fix of his jaw as he left the hospital with his sister-in-law and nephew to wait for a call that might now come too late. The navy eyes were hidden behind dark glasses, yet nothing could shield from Amelia the depth of his despair, the pain behind the 'no comments', the agony of her apparent betrayal.

And Amelia was as guilty as the rest of the general public—greedy for insight, surfing news bulletins, listening avidly as reporters explained the disease that afflicted his nephew, that Vaughan Mason himself might carry the gene. She learnt that even in his apparent anger, his seeming withdrawal after their love-making, Vaughan had been concerned for *her*—had somehow been trying to protect her.

He *had* loved her. With torturous hindsight she knew that now—knew that in his own unique, special way Vaughan Mason had truly adored her.

The loud ringing of her doorbell only made Amelia jump. The prospect of another visitor did nothing to raise her spirits, and she didn't want another bouquet or congratulations she didn't deserve. And anyway her apartment already looked like a funeral parlor— felt like a funeral parlor.

Amelia didn't want to see anyone.

Unless it was Vaughan, standing grey and washed-out in her doorway, looking as awful as she felt, yet the most beautiful thing she could ever hope to see.

'You look awful.' Perhaps not the most romantic of greetings, but it was all her quivering lips could manage. She braced herself for the crash landing of his temper, another hit to her bruised and battered heart.

'Turbulence.'

She blinked as he managed a wan smile, still scarcely able to believe he was here, unable to comprehend that he didn't appear angry. Surely after the hell he'd been through these past days he should be raging? But instead he was talking almost normally— completely unable to meet her eyes, of course, but fairly normally all the same.

'Bloody turbulence all the way from Melbourne.'

'Turbulence?'

'Did I forget to tell you that I'm terrified of flying?' He didn't even soften it with a dry smile, and Amelia closed her eyes in another second of regret. The ritual trip to the newsagent made sense now, and the white-knuckled silence in helicopters. She was glimpsing again the softer side of the wonderful man that she could have had.

'How's Jamie?' Still holding the door for support, Amelia asked one of the many questions that had been plaguing her. 'How's he dealing with all the publicity? And Liza…?'

'They're fine,' Vaughan said slowly. 'They're dealing with it. In fact it's almost a relief that it's out in the open now. Almost,' he added, and Amelia knew it still must hurt.

But suddenly the conversation shifted, suddenly they were talking about them—or at least Vaughan was.

'Amelia, I don't care.' Dragging her into his arms, he held her fiercely, breathing in the scent of her hair, holding her as if for support, and all she could do was hold him back, words strangling in her throat as he loved her for all the wrong reasons. 'I don't care just as long as we can move on—I can see why you did it, why you had to go for the story. It's your job, Amelia,'

'You don't understand…'

'No, but I'm trying to.'

Pulling his head back, he held her cheeks, kissed her parted lips, drinking from them as if they were the life force he needed, as if her kiss, her embrace, was the one thing that could make him go on. But she pulled back, his touch desperately wanted but the truth needed more.

'Vaughan, I need you to see something.' Letting him go even for a second was a feat in itself, but somehow she managed, somehow she made it to her desk. She rummaged through the appalling mess and for the second time in their short relationship held her breath as he read a piece of work with her name upon it—only this time it was the truth. Each word was laced with the esteem in which she held him, each carefully crafted sentence a pure deliverance of the truth.

'This is what I filed, Vaughan. This is the piece I wrote.'

'I guess I should have had more faith.'

'Yes, Vaughan, you should.' Something in her voice made him look up. 'Vaughan, how you can say that you love me when you think I did that to you defies explanation. It wasn't me. It never was me. Apparently one of the other mothers in Jamie's ward tipped off the press—that's why Carter was following you; that's why they jumped so high at the chance of my spending a week with you. They thought they were on to a big story. This woman thought that her son was sicker than Jamie, that Jamie was somehow getting preferential treatment because of who his uncle was, so she—'

'Poor woman!'

His reaction confused her. She'd expected some of the venom he'd directed at her when he'd thought she'd betrayed him to somehow appear again. But not for the first time she marvelled at his insight, at the hidden depths behind this amazing man.

'When you're desperate you'll do anything. I'd probably have done the same.'

'I've tried to get the paper to print a retraction.' Amelia shrugged her shoulders helplessly. 'Perhaps if we both lean on Paul…'

'There's no need.' Vaughan shook his head. 'Jamie's still where he should be on the transplant list, despite the news coverage. Those doctors have stood firm. It takes more than a newspaper article to scare those guys, Amelia. They face death every day.' His eyes found hers. 'I'm sorry, Amelia, more sorry than you know for doubting you. I've just been so used to being let down, so used to being misquoted just to grab a headline. But when I thought it was you I lost my head for a while. I was so angry I couldn't think straight…'

'Touché,' Amelia blushed, thinking of her bitch-on-heels act at his hotel door.

'Yet even with the hell of these last few days, Amelia, all I could think about was you—the real you I was sure I'd seen. Despite the agony, despite the accusations, all I could think was that if I never got to see you again you were the only thing in this world I'd truly miss.'

'Apart from your family,' Amelia said softly. Though it was the one thing with Vaughan that didn't need saying. She had seen the love that lay burning behind the 'no comment'.

'Apart from my family,' Vaughan confirmed. 'I just wanted to protect Jamie. I didn't want the papers to get hold of it. I'd promised my brother and Liza I'd keep Jamie out of the public eye. But I knew if we were ever going to move forward then I'd have to tell you. When I heard you say that babies were firmly entrenched on your list…' The frown on his forehead deepened. 'I carry the gene, Amelia…'

'I'd already worked that out. That's why you over-reacted when you found out I wasn't on the pill, wasn't it?' Amelia took his hand in hers. 'I should have known, Vaughan. It was beyond irresponsible…'

'I'm sorry.' He swallowed hard. 'I'm always careful—*always*,' he emphasized. 'I was more angry with myself than you—couldn't believe I'd let myself get so carried away. And after you said at lunch that nothing on your list was negligible I figured that was it—that there wasn't any point. I never thought it would go any further until….' The beginnings of a smile ghosted on his lips. 'You have a very good knack for making me lose my head, Amelia.'

'I know,' Amelia replied—because she did. She knew for the first time in her life the reckless abandonment that came hand in hand with love.

'If you carry the gene too…'

'Let's not worry about that now.'

'We have to. Because if you feel even a tenth of what I do then it's something we're going to have to face. Nothing on your list's negotiable, Amelia. You want the lot. And if I can't give you everything…'

'It's the top of the list that matters most…' His eyes were holding hers, days of pain slowly drifting away as she spoke from the bottom of her heart. 'Safety,' she said softly. 'The safety of always being loved, knowing that no matter what I do, no matter how bad it seems, I've always got you to lean on.'

'You do,' Vaughan said simply, kissing her on her waiting lips, affirming the desire that blazed in his eyes. 'So what happens now?' A smile inched over his face. 'Does this mean I'm finally ready to settle down?'

'No way,' Amelia answered, enjoying the tiny moment of confusion in his loving eyes. 'I have it from an extremely reliable source that you don't believe in settling down! I don't have my notes, of course, so you'll forgive me if I misquote…'

'I already did,' Vaughan drawled, raining tiny kisses on her face.

His hand toying with the hem of her skirt was making it terribly hard to concentrate.

'But I believe "hotting up" was your appalling choice of phrase. In fact, I'm sure you said something about hardly being able to keep your hands off the very lucky woman.'

'No.' Vaughan grinned. 'I think you're taking it out of context.'

'I can always get my notes,' Amelia gasped, as the hand that had been toying grew rather more insistent.

Making to stand up, she heard his moan of frustration as he pulled her back down.

'Damned journalists,' Vaughan whispered in her ear. 'Well, I suppose if you've got it in writing then I'm just going to have to stand by it. I guess I'm going to have to spend the rest of my life living up to my lousy, oversexed, completely insatiable reputation.'

'Yes,' Amelia gasped again. A witty response was on the tip of her tongue, but so too was Vaughan, and coherence flew out of the window. 'Yes, please.'

EPILOGUE

SAFE.

Peering out of the window as Vaughan's car pulled into the driveway, as he climbed out and retrieved his computer and briefcase, she knew that this time there was no sliver of detriment behind the word, no question of settling for second best as there had been when she had first voiced it.

He made her feel safe.

Safe enough to shoot for the stars, safe enough to go too far, safe enough to be herself, knowing he was always beside her, was always there, proudly ready to catch her if ever she fell.

'Hey!' That delicious smile greeted her, but his eyes didn't hold hers, searching instead for the baby she held in her arms—his reward to come home to after a long day in the office. And she watched her resident tycoon, supposed playboy, scoop the precious bundle into strong arms, shower a giggling gummy face with kisses, before planting a slower more deliberate one on Amelia. 'God, I've missed you two.'

And she knew that he had.

Knew with complete conviction that wherever his work took him, whoever he met along the way, his heart was always with his family.

'How's Rory been?'

'Grizzly,' Amelia replied, rolling her eyes. She put

her son down, his fat legs circling the air, and he gave out tiny unprovoked giggles, looking anything but.

'His mother too?' Vaughan grinned and Amelia pursed her lips, knowing what was coming next and deciding to get in first.

'I'm not bored,' Amelia insisted. 'I love being a stay-at-home mum.'

'He's got teeth, Amelia,' Vaughan pointed out. 'And if I remember rightly that was about the time Maria decided to come back to work and put you out of a job.'

'She didn't put me out of a job,' Amelia retorted. 'I'd already handed in my notice. After the way they treated you it was the last place I wanted to be.'

'But you miss it, though,' Vaughan said perceptively. 'Miss using that crazy brain of yours.'

'I like being with Rory.'

'Of course you do, and that's the beauty of your work—you can do it from home, set the world alight right here from our lounge.' He watched two spots of colour burn on her cheeks and completely misconstrued them. 'Amelia, you can write the pieces you really want to now. It's not as if we need the money. If nobody buys them it won't matter a scrap.'

'It will matter to me.' She watched as his eyes narrowed, flushed some more under his scrutiny.

'I don't need to persuade you to work again, do I?'

Amelia shook her head, pulling a few rather well-thumbed pieces of paper from under a sofa cushion and nibbling on the skin around her thumb as Vaughan read through them.

'This is great, Amelia.' Hearing the admiration in

his voice, Amelia remembered to breathe, knowing Vaughan's appraisal would be honest. 'Why didn't you tell me you were interviewing Mr Hassan?'

'I wanted to be sure I could still do it,' Amelia admitted honestly. 'I wanted to be sure I could do his work justice.'

'And you have,' Vaughan said simply, and she could hear the emotion in his voice, see the flash of what could possibly be tears in those navy eyes. 'I know sometimes I get a bit pumped up with my own self-importance, but what that guy does for a living—well, it kind of puts things into perspective…'

His voice trailed off and Amelia knew he was struggling, knew he was recalling the agonising days before, during and after Jamie's transplant—the miracle they had all been granted under the skilful hands of Mr Hassan.

'It's brilliant—your article's perfect. This is going to really help awareness. The only trouble is now you're going to have to top it. You're going to have to think of something just as interesting to write about…' A knowing smile inched across his lips as Amelia for once remained silent, those two spots of colour spreading across her face and down her neck.

'Amelia? Are you going to tell me what you're up to?'

Back under the sofa cushion, she pulled out some more papers—only this time photos were attached, dark almond eyes were staring back at him, and she watched his curious frown, his mouth opening to speak and closing again.

Amelia tentatively tried to explain. Tried to explain

to this wonderful, difficult man how she was feeling, tried to capture with halting words that the more love she received the more she had to give, that love really was the cup that runneth over.

'You remember when I stalled on taking the blood test? Remember how terrified I was that I might carry the gene as well?'

'Of course,' Vaughan said warily.

'And you remember how we decided that if we weren't going to have children then we'd consider overseas adoption, and you got all the information, showed me how many children there were in need of loving parents?'

'Mmm.'

'Well, I was thinking of doing a piece on that— thinking of following a couple on their journey.'

'Good idea!' Vaughan grinned, relief evident on his face. 'So who did you have in mind?'

His relief was short-lived, his eyes widening when Amelia didn't answer, just stared at the photo he was holding in his hands—a two-year-old boy who, according to the bio, quite simply couldn't be placed. Newborn babes were the order of the day for most young couples. Two-year-olds with attitude were far harder to find a home for.

'If we'd ended up adopting we'd have loved him.' Amelia swallowed hard. 'We'd have loved him just as much as we love Rory. He wouldn't have been second best.'

'No.' Vaughan raked a hand through his hair. 'But, Amelia, he might already have a family by now.'

'And he might not.'

For the longest time he was silent, staring at the photo for an age before turning to her. 'Are you unhappy, Amelia? Is there…?'

'I've never been more happy, Vaughan. Never been more fulfilled. Over and over I pinch myself—can't believe how lucky I am, how lucky we all are to have found each other.'

She knew he was listening, but his eyes had left hers now, were staring instead at the sad, bewildered eyes in the picture he held. A soft smile formed on his lips. 'He is kind of cute,' Vaughan said very slowly, very cautiously, and Amelia knew she had to hold back a touch, couldn't let her mounting excitement sway him for even a moment. This decision was way too important to be rushed into. It was a child they were talking about, not some crazy impulse buy they could take back and exchange if things didn't work out.

But already she loved him.

And from the look in Vaughan's eyes, the way his thumb was stroking the pale cheeks on the photo, he was starting to feel that way too.

'I'm supposed to be a bastard.' Putting down the papers, he dragged her into his arms and she went unrelenting. 'I'm supposed to be a complete cad, making a mere token effort to settle down.'

'I know.' Amelia smiled, closing her eyes in bliss as he held her ever closer to his chest. 'I read all about it last week.'

'You know,' Vaughan whispered, pulling her in, safe in the warm glow of love, 'this is going to completely ruin my reputation.'

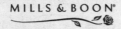

MILLS & BOON

DARK
SEDUCTIONS
Submit to his pleasure...

ANNE
MATHER

ROBYN
DONALD

SARA
CRAVEN

On sale 2nd September 2005

Available at most branches of WHSmith, Tesco, ASDA, Martins,
Borders, Eason, Sainsbury's and all good paperback bookshops.

FREE

4 BOOKS AND A SURPRISE GIFT!

We would like to take this opportunity to thank you for reading this Mills & Boon® book by offering you the chance to take FOUR more specially selected titles from the Modern Romance™ series absolutely FREE! We're also making this offer to introduce you to the benefits of the Reader Service™—

- ★ **FREE home delivery**
- ★ **FREE gifts and competitions**
- ★ **FREE monthly Newsletter**
- ★ **Books available before they're in the shops**
- ★ **Exclusive Reader Service offers**

Accepting these FREE books and gift places you under no obligation to buy; you may cancel at any time, even after receiving your free shipment. Simply complete your details below and return the entire page to the address below. You don't even need a stamp!

YES! Please send me 4 free Modern Romance books and a surprise gift. I understand that unless you hear from me, I will receive 6 superb new titles every month for just £2.75 each, postage and packing free. I am under no obligation to purchase any books and may cancel my subscription at any time. The free books and gift will be mine to keep in any case.

P5ZEE

Ms/Mrs/Miss/Mr...Initials ....
BLOCK CAPITALS PLEASE

Surname ....

Address ....

....

....Postcode ....

Send this whole page to:
The Reader Service, FREEPOST CN81, Croydon, CR9 3WZ